WALKING ON RIPPLES

The Angling Life

David Murphy

The Liffey Press

Published by
The Liffey Press Ltd
Raheny Shopping Centre, Second Floor
Raheny, Dublin 5, Ireland
www.theliffeypress.com

A catalogue record of this book is
available from the British Library.

ISBN 978-1-908308-61-0

Some of the stories in *Walking on Ripples* previously
appeared in *Broken Heroes, Dark Visions, FTL, Lost
Notes* and *Phoenix Irish Short Stories*.

Printed in Ireland by Sprint-Print.

Items should be returned on or before the last date shown below. Items not already requested by other borrowers may be renewed in person, in writing or by telephone. To renew, please quote the number on the barcode label. To renew online a PIN is required. This can be requested at your local library.
Renew online @ **www.dublincitypubliclibraries.ie**
Fines charged for overdue items will include postage incurred in recovery. Damage to or loss of items will be charged to the borrower.

Leabharlanna Poiblí Chathair Bhaile Átha Cliath
Dublin City Public Libraries

Baile Átha Cliath
Dublin City

Central Library, Henry Street
An Lárleabharlann, Sráid Annraoi
Tel: 8734333

Date Due	Date Due	Date Due
0 4 IAN 2016		

About the Author

David Murphy's previous books include *Broken Heroes* (short stories, 1995); *Alienations* (short stories, 1998); *Arkon Chronicles* (novella, 2003); *Lost Notes* (short stories, 2004); *Longevity City* (novel, 2005); and *Bird of Prey* (novella, 2011). He was born in Cork but has lived north of Dublin, and in Waterford, for many years. This is his first work featuring nonfiction. For more information, see the author's website at www.davidmurph.wordpress.com.

Contents

For
Marie, Barry & Claire
and for Isobel

1

The Hills of Donegal

Fish are creatures hooked on memory. Fish are triggers to unleash the past. With their noses they eke out memories buried deep in silt. Unknown to us, they use their heads to nudge those distant, half-forgotten, half-submerged, parts of the human mind.

Memories of a boy in third class; aged about nine. He stood on the concrete path of the Lough, a wildlife sanctuary on the then southern flank of Cork city. Guarding his net in one hand, bucket in the other, the boy looked up at a man rich enough to own his own fishing rod. He answered the tall man's question by saying that his primary schoolteacher in Sully's Quay was a Mr O'Sullivan.

"Mr O'Sullivan? Ah, you mean Fuzzy!" The angler laughed in a sing-song accent before reeling in yet another roach on a ball of dough. "Fuzzy was my teacher, too."

The boy brought home a bucketful of five roach donated by the angler. He put them in a makeshift pond: a large, ten-gallon, plastic, rectangular container that once carried chemicals. The fish did not survive long in such a hazardous environment. He watched them die: first one, then another and another until all were dead.

Not long after their demise, the nine-year-old's father constructed a circular pond about four feet in diameter, roughly eight inches deep – an improvement on the chemical container but far from an ideal home for fish. Bad enough that it was made of household bricks cemented together, and too shallow. The pond lacked living plants and therefore clouded over every couple of weeks after cleaning. Poorly aerated, oxygen-starved water is not conducive to good fish-keeping. The pond was stocked with goldfish from a pet shop on North Main Street, at least two of the fish surviving many years. When the water froze in those harsh winters, the boy tackled the problem by smashing the ice with thunderous belts of his hurley, oblivious to the harmful shockwaves this sent reverberating throughout the pond. That pair of goldfish may have had longevity on their side but they might also have gone prematurely deaf – and may have been startled by the occasional Airfix model warship floating experimentally on the surface.

The roundy pond's main supply source was the Lough. A stock of thorneen, pinkeen, redbreast (minnow and stickleback) caught by the million by the boy with his net. Occasionally, he landed small silver fish the identification of which was beyond him. These were probably roach fry – they never lasted long. Now and then he caught thorneens by angling with a worm on a piece of string. Once, on the road-side of the Lough, he glimpsed movement in a weed bed and followed the swaying trail with his net, resulting in the triumphant landing of a roach – a leviathan, so it seemed. For the boy, the attraction of fishing was by now set as firmly as a hook.

Even an assault, months later, by a gang of thuggish older boys failed to deter him from his love of fishing. They may have robbed him of his bar of Cadbury's, and thrown his net and jar into the water, and jeered at him as all his thorneens escaped, but the jar contained a smaller, lidded jar that housed a crimson redbreast, glorious in his mating colours, which the boy retrieved.

There were forays to the Tramore River: a fresh, pristine stream that ran east about three-quarter ways between the Lough and the bed of the old Cork-Bandon Railway track. The small boy once landed a bizarre, black, unidentifiable fish of about four inches long. Other boys dammed the Tramore in summertime to create swimming pools of crystal clean waters. Nowadays, the Tramore River is a sad reflection of its former life. Nobody swims, or fishes, in it any more. Coralled and piped by concrete roads, bypass bridges, and the epitome of hellish modern ways – the suburban retail unit – it flows filthy and dead, testimony to progress unbound. The railway trackbed that would have made a fine light-rail route for the south side of Cork is now a road.

The Tramore River turned out to be a sideline, a temporary distraction. The sea may have sparkled and jigged a salty lure across a child's mind in faraway Crosshaven and other exotic places, the River Lee may have flowed only a mile away – a mile is a big distance for small legs. None of these things mattered. The Lough was Eden, the Lough was Valhalla. Golden scales of unattainable carp rolled and wallowed on its surface like hippopotami on misty summer school mornings as the sun broke through – the sight of them eased the pain of horrors that lay ahead under the leather strap of the Christian Brothers in Sully's Quay. Not that these horrors unfolded just yet.

The boy would be in fourth class before he witnessed a ten-year-old called Liam being hammered and slapped around the small, cramped classroom for an hour beneath the cold-eyed glare of a statue of the Child of Prague. Liam had composed a little composition about two pet cats, Whitie and Darkie, but had made the mistake of adding the sentence: 'Darkie is the Mrs' – an unpardonable sexual reference in the eyes of a Brother, one that merited three things: a brief and tense silence, an atavistic glare and an explosive battering – the lifting of the lid on a pressure-cooker of bigotry, guilt and abuse of power.

Classmates gathered around Liam in the yard at eleven o'clock breaktime, a bunch of ten-year-olds innocent and angry yet unsure what to do except advise their classmate to go home, to not go back upstairs. The urgings of his schoolmates failed to dissuade Liam from returning to class – a strange blend of dread and dutiful acceptance glinted in the young boy's fate-strangled eyes as he trudged warily up the cruel steps to the classroom on the third floor for another hour of digs, pokes, slaps, hair-pulling and name-calling.

Two years later, in sixth class on a sunny Friday afternoon, another Brother warned, "God help ye if Cork don't win on Sunday."

The team from Cork were beaten.

The following Monday morning the chalky scent of fear hung like dust motes in musky classroom air. The Brother standing in front of the blackboard loosened the belt on his tunic so he could swing his right arm better. A few practice arcs at the head of the class to free up the muscles, like an axe-man swinging his arm to limber up before the execution to make sure he wielded the power of the arc just right. Then two dozen boys received two hard belts of the leather strap on each hand. So much for instilling a love of hurling. So much for education.

These events still lay ahead of the nine-year-old third class pupil as he skipped down the hill from Lough Church – a building tall and imposing as all city churches at the time; symbol of religious duty that hung about our necks; a cankerous carapace on our collar bones; the font of all knowledge and righteousness; the one, true, holy and apostolic church – down the hill from that and to the right the welcome sight of swans gliding in like seaplanes borrowing the overhead flight-path to the nearby airport. Honking as they crash-landed, creating huge bow waves. The Lough teemed with crazy coots and busy little moorhens, though these days it has a greater selection of exotic ducks than it had back in the 1960s.

The water once froze so severely children and adults ventured out to slide over the fish beneath. How odd the soles of shoes must seem to a fish's eye looking up. Photographs of that remarkable freeze of 1963 adorn the walls of the nearby Hawthorn Bar. With surrounding trees and grassy parkland, the Lough was – still is – a magical, idyllic place. All the small boy needed was to have his imagination fed on tales of monstrous castles that once stood in the middle of the lake, but sank beneath. Rising out of the water is an island Amazonian to the eyes of a child; dark and sinister-looking, the perfect home for a sunken castle. The boy's grandfather nurtured him on those tales. Between tales above and tails below, the boy was hooked. Who knew what treasures a scoop of the net might bring? No matter that the carp were uncatchable. No matter that the roach that swam beneath may, in fact, have been rudd. No matter that the small boy's targets were modest: thorneen, pinkeen, redbreast. No matter that father, grandfather, Fuzzy O'Sullivan and (probably) the angler, are now dead. No matter that young Liam took a beating in fourth class – I hope fate has dealt him a kind hand in the many days since those dark years. What really matters is this: the hook was set.

The hook fell out as soon as teenage years arrived. Bait was taken once again many summers later. Fast forward more than twenty years to Mountcharles Pier about four miles west of Donegal town: Gerry handed over a rod and showed the boy, now a man, how to close and open the gate on the reel when casting. Five pollack offered themselves up. Not only the rod, but also the die, was well and truly cast.

Mountcharles Pier is a wonderful viewing platform, the prow of a static cruiser. Donegal Bay sweeps majestically out to sea. To the left, the tide rushes in through the rip-roaring Hassan's, on past St Ernan's, Bell Island, and stops only where the River Eske flows down through the town. Across the waves, the lofty sand dunes of Murvagh. Miles down the coast, Mulloughmore. Away to the south, the hazy blue outline of the coast of Mayo. Beyond that, on clear days, the unmistakable peak of Croagh Patrick. Nearer the shore, brightly painted boats and lobster pot flags bob on red and orange moorings. Oar-weed, kelp and bladder-weed drift in on Atlantic swells that break gently, sometimes not so gently, on the rocky shore around the pier. What more could an angler want?

A painting of a favourite hotspot for one thing. A fine-art shop called Miller Print once traded on the Diamond in Donegal town. I fell in love with a painting hanging there, an oil on canvas of Mountcharles Pier. The asking price was hefty for the time, a bit too much for the pocket of a schoolteacher. Two hundred and fifty pounds.

"Would you take two hundred?"

"Oh, I don't know," said the shop assistant. "We'd have to ask the artist about that."

I never pursued the painting. One of the regrets of my life that I let it go. The shop is gone, too. The last time I looked, it had morphed into a boutique, a sad portent of things to come in end-of-millennium Ireland. Is there anything else an angler might want? A little more room at the end of the pier would do no harm. Two is comfortable, three a squeeze, four ...?

Three years on from those five pollack taken on a borrowed rod, I stood at the end of the pier with Barry on a typical summer's evening – breezy, overcast, more than a hint of rain. Our luck was out, like the fish. We had our own rods now, but nothing was taking. Two German tourists arrived, bristling with big rods and heavy tackle. They squeezed in alongside us. Four reels made tight work of the fishing. Casting became a restricted chore. After a while one of the tourists guffawed, "Three of us here and no fish. Well," he added, "three and a half, actually. Har! Har!"

That did not go down well with us; the half he referred to being the nine-year-old – the incredible symmetry of life – who stood alongside me. After much muttering, we had the last laugh: the half went on to land the only catch of the evening, a solitary pollack.

There is more to Mountcharles than the promise of a single species. Over the years, Barry and I have hauled in mackerel as well as pollack on feather and sprat lure. Fish can be plentiful when conditions are right at Mountcharles, but undoubtedly the local magnet for pollack macho-fishing is John's Point, a jutting finger of skinny headland that points for miles out into the deep heart of the bay. Head seaward off the road between Inver and Dunkineely. Drive, or cycle, to the lighthouse. On the way, pass rocks indented with fossils, a crumbling old castle, a cove called Trabawn where white sands and blue waters glitter like the Tropics when the sun shines. Giant pollack live in the deeps off the rocks near the lighthouse. Be warned, bring strong tackle and stronger arms. Nothing can beat the sensation of a four pound pollack taking a sprat lure – on a fly rod! It's also a great spot to float-fish for wrasse. Barry lifted three one day on floating limpet. I once saw a whale roll in the waves just offshore, but Barry was busy keeping an eye on the wrasse bubble-float, and did not believe me when I told him what I'd witnessed. I've also taken mackerel and pollack from other coastal locations in the county, from a heaving boat off Doorin near Blind Rock (not long after the exploits of the Irish soccer team in Italia '90) to as far north as Portsalon.

A great asset in fishing's favour is that it's not weather-dependent, a boon when you're in a location prone to the wind and rain of Atlantic weather systems – typical Donegal summer weather. Years of cycling and golfing had proved frustrating in the extreme. It always seemed to rain. Wet wheel rims and sopping golf clubs. Fishing felt like a Godsend. If too wet to go out on a bike or play a round of golf, don cap and jacket and head to where rain is a blessing. The rivers were waiting, brimming with the promise of a feeding frenzy after spate-time. Under Tawnawully Bridge on the Lowrymore, near the new road bridge on the Abbey River, just upstream of Aghadullagh Bridge on the Ballintra, under the road over the Bridgetown – all these rivers yielded small brown trout on various flies: Greenwell's Glory, Willie Gunn, silver-black salmon flies. On the Abbey, a little brownie on the second cast of a fly. Then nothing for the rest of the day. The Murvagh River surrendered, of all things, an eel on ledgered worm just upstream of the bridge. The larger and more famous waters – River Eske and Eany More – proved equally productive.

We paid visits to a secret spot high on the Eany, above Drumboarty Bridge. Local brown trout could not resist Butcher, Blue Dun and Greenwell's flies dangled in front of their inquisitive noses. We drove there two days in a row and discovered a tiddler caught on a fly we had abandoned in brambles overnight. Levels had gone down enough the following day to make wading feasible, so I made my way carefully to the bushes where I could see the line glisten in sunshine. Something in the way the line moved had alerted me – a tiny brown trout, freshly hooked. The day had only started, yielding two small wildies for Claire. The Eske also gave us plenty of wild ones, fingerlings mainly, in super locations such as Miss Jenny's Bridge, the Mill Hole and Gorrell's Bridge. Barry took two small brownies on floating worm near the dam, and another one on the fly near the bypass bridge. Black Pennell, Cow Dung and Willie Gunn flies seemed to work best there, along with the usual fly assortment from other Donegal rivers.

Above where rivers flow broad and deep, mountains stand tall and steep. In the foothills of the Blue Stacks are the best-kept, most alluringly beautiful and stunning of Ireland's fishing secrets: Donegal mountain loughs. These are no places for record seekers or trophy hunters with keep-nets and weighing scales in their eager hands. Peaty qualities of mountain water prevent trout from growing much. They may be small but most certainly they are not stunted. Superb specimens, one and all – sleek and colourful and, when you land one big enough for breakfast, they taste of salmon. First you have to find their homes in the hills of Donegal. Some of the loughs are remote and difficult to get to. Ordnance Survey maps, sturdy boots, a love of hillwalking, are minimum requirements. Best tell someone where you're going and when to expect you back – in case a treacherous bog-hole claims a human victim.

In the second edition of *Loughs of Ireland,* published in 1992, Peter O'Reilly described one of these loughs as "remote, peaceful and very beautiful". The water he referred to is Lough Golagh, seven miles northeast of Donegal town, high up off the Ballybofey road near Barnesmore Gap. Those adjectives that once applied to Golagh sadly no longer fit the description. Now Golagh is arrived at quite easily via a gouged-out access road built to accommodate diggers and machinery required to bring up, and erect, huge wind turbines that tower over the water like preying beasts. They create a whining noise that, combined with fading evening light, is enough to discourage even the most enthusiastic angler. Believe me, I was there one evening and caught a solitary little brownie before the turbines scared me so much with their noise, even just their eerie and unnatural presence, that I scarpered off downhill as fast as I could.

One of the best loughs, like many such things, turned out to be our first. Lough Nadarragh is cheek to jowl with the Donegal-Pettigo road. Access is not a problem; the lough even boasts a small lakeside car-park. In August it also boasts an evening rise that you can set your watch by. From the road bridge Barry and I took five perch on the worm. We returned a couple of evenings later, this time plodding around to the northern shore where, using teams of three or four wet flies (Heather Moth being a local speciality) strung out from bubble floats, we caught another perch. More importantly, we landed three trout including one particularly respectable one. The trout were so free-rising supper was guaranteed. The only downside were the midges. If Lough Nadarragh's midges are lacking in anything, it is not persistence.

That proved to be the first lough in a whole necklace of pearls garnered over many years, mountain jewels with hypnotic names – Lough Avehy, Lough Unshin, Lough Awaddy, Lough Namanfin, Rath Lough, Lough Eske, Lough Croagh, Glencoagh Lough, Glen Lough, Trumman and St Peter's Lough. Not all yielded trout. From Avehy a big fat roach on floating worm. Out of dark Trumman a pike so thunderous in the shallows Pepé felt unable to contain his barking at the strange disturbance in the water. He patrolled the water's edge for ages afterwards, ears alert for the sound of another monster doing loop-the-loops in front of his disbelieving doggy eyes. Remind me not to use a three-pronged German Sprat on a pike again. One hook is kinder. From the north-western end of Lough Namanfin, a small sea trout, silver with the promise of the ocean. From Rath Lough two perch on Greenwell's Glory and Butcher flies, a sad pair of portents of what was to come.

Before the sadness, joy of grassing three fighting brownies after arm-wrenching torpedo runs from the eastern and southern shores of Unshin on a warm summer's day. Another fish, another summer: that stillness in the air at Croagh, despite the north-easterly. Anticipation, the promise of a line cutting a capital V through clear mountain water. Flash of fin sparkled on the surface over by the reeds, the tug on the rod. I can still feel the gentle pull of something wild and wonderful.

After five fruitless hours on the shore of Lough Eske, a pair of brownies on a Wickham's Fancy in a north wind. At last, following four fishless hours at St Peter's Lough, a one-and-a-half pounder that fought so hard in the twilight rise I was unable to use the net, opting instead to beach him on the carpark shore. The pleasure of a little Northern Ireland wildie caught on a Blue Dun floated from the Fermanagh shore of border-straddling Lough Awaddy – a good place to stop on the way from Dublin; what a welcome to Donegal, as good as the "Donegal Welcomes You" sign hanging in the fuchsia hedgerow on the roadside outside Pettigo. Not to mention a nice brownie in a north-westerly at Glencoagh – what made it all the sweeter was that my previous visits to this little lough had ended fishless.

And sweeter still the pint afterwards in Melly's or John Rock's or McCafferty's. Or drinks and always warm company later in the Abbey Hotel where a welcome from Dom was guaranteed, and where, later still, the sun would sometimes rise. What better the morning after than to stock up on flies in Charlie Doherty's Tackle Shop, an old front room premises so small you could not swing a five-foot rod in it, but what a treasure house of tackle, friendliness and knowledge.

And then the sorrow – first experienced in the Pullans, that mystical, hilly, moorland plateau between Laghy and Pettigo. Sunlight never glared here. Heat did not oppress, though rain often drenched. Anticipation always mounted as the road levelled out over mountaintop. No sickly smell of tarry surfaces – instead, the sweet and fragrant smell of bog. Air magical, light implacable, mountains magisterial as they punched the warm air up and away. I have travelled this plateau in all seasons and never been less than awed by it. The view always breathtaking; proper mountain moorland. No towering trees blocked the roadside. Here were scrub-trees, mountain ash and holly. Clumps of branches forever buckled and bowed to the wind. You could look out over burrs and bushes, streams and mountains and see loughs where sunlight lay down in great sparkling sheets. Mounds of bog rose on both sides but fell away quickly enough, often enough, to reveal a landscape so desolate there was no sign of human habitation anywhere. Desolation enough for loneliness.

The road had magic in the old days, and still does though you need to know when and where to look. Up around the sharp bend after the turn-off for Lough Keeran and Killeter, the road pulls a trick out of its gravelly mountain hat. Up, up the road twists around a giant rock. Suddenly, it opens up the most evocative view in the whole world, never failing to remind me of an old song about a valley where the sun always shines. Then the road jack-knifes – almost on purpose as if to veer your windscreen and your pair of beady eyes away from the paradise just glimpsed.

I have seen this valley in all kinds of weather. In summer sunsets with the sky tinted lilac, mountains painted pink. Even in deepest grey of winter, through mist and fog and rain, the sun always shone. On crispy days frosty drumlins define the valley with the sparkle of best December childhood. The valley twinkles even in a blizzard, though you can't beat a hazy, lazy mix of early summer and evening's declining light. The view from high up perfect; a wide, sweeping bend gives ample time to gaze down on another ribbon of meandering road glinting along the valley floor. Where that road is going I do not know but have always meant to find out. In my imagination it was, and still is, a wondrous road, a wizard's road, a yellow brick road; a ribbon of rutted country lane – straight out of the Haywain – that twists and turns from foreground to vanishing point.

Two cottages, thatched and white-washed, stood at the head of the valley. One always had a red tractor parked outside, partially hidden by an island of rhododendrons. The other housed a little white caravan in the lee of its gable end. The cottages seemed a tad fanciful, as if this were a painting and the cottages added to the landscape as a flourish by the last of the great romanticists. On tranquil autumn days wispy chimney smoke rose from the cottages as though the copper-coloured valley warmed its innards for cooler days ahead. There are trees, too. Real trees, not scrub ones. Sheep graze the valley walls and yes, the grass was greener, but when the sorrow came, it was twofold.

Firstly, the magic and the views have disappeared from the Pullans because of a modern affliction: whole forests of tamed, lamentable pines. Christmas trees are bland and boring, but can they grow on bogland! Soldiers look fine and natural in regimented lines. Trees? Broadleaf forests are lush and natural gifts of creation, unlike these sitka plantations with barren under-growth good for nothing except carpets of pine needles and wood-money for some rich man's purse. I drive faster up here now. There is less to look at. I glance occasionally from side to side, searching for something to break the monotony of battalion after battalion of fir and spruce. It's a long time since I've seen a monstrous peat machine through a gap in the trees, glinting in the setting sun, almost invisible in its lair. That machine always lurked around here, clinging to the side of one hill or another, like one of those giant spindly things from *War of the Worlds*. It certainly looked Martian: six rusty-yellow legs rising to a control cabin at least five metres off the ground. Never less than fascinating, an incredible machine, an arachnophobe's nightmare digging up the turf. Such a machine is a natural, if man-made, thing to see in a bog. Christmas trees? Never.

And then the second barb slung on sorrow's deadly hook. We had our first inkling of it in Rath Lough. A pair of greedy perch on two separate flies, Greenwell's Glory and a Butcher. No trout. Another manifestation from the shallows of Glen Lough – a perch on a silver-black, two-pronged fly. Not a trout to be seen, serving only to confirm suspicions that certain people, mainly Northern European holiday-home owners, have, allegedly, deliberately introduced predator fish, perch and pike, to mountain loughs and water systems because they like to catch them for the larders of their kitchens. Rumours also abound of continental tourists driving around in camper vans, cool-boxes and mobile fridges bursting with pike, a delicacy to certain palates, to take back home on the car ferries. These pike-introductions started in the sixties or seventies, gaining momentum in the eighties and nineties. Allegedly. The entire business might seem funny and harmless. It is neither.

In that bible for Irish fishermen and fisherwomen, the fourth edition of Peter O'Reilly's *Loughs of Ireland*, published in 2007, which Barry kindly bought that year as a Christmas present, bodies of water lovingly and painstakingly described in earlier editions are reduced to the following grim, disheartening passage. O'Reilly lists a dozen loughs, one beneath the other like an inscription on a tombstone, including four of those outlined above. They are:

Lough Avehy
Glen Lough
Rath Lough
Lough Unshin

Beneath this graveyard-like inscription, he writes, quoting from earlier notes:

> *... our conversations about them contain phrases like "free rising ½lb brown trout", "very popular lake", "really excellent 1lb trout", "provides great fishing early morning and late in the evening", "lovely golden trout", "good quality brown trout fishing – remarkably good", "can give great sport", "good brown trout and a lovely sandy shore" and "seventy-five percent of the bank is fishable".*
>
> *Let that be their obituary – lovely places destroyed. Today they are a monument to those who so carelessly, perhaps maliciously, maybe in ignorance, but certainly selfishly introduced pike initially, and then rudd and other coarse fish. A part of our indigenous, natural environment that existed for ten thousand years, is lost forever.*

And that is appropriate, for that description is indeed an obituary.

Luckily, not all Donegal loughs have been ravaged by imported pike. Perhaps the most remarkable and, in my case, inspirational lough is situated high in a remote place, well off the beaten track and hard to get to. For the purpose of this book its location remains a closely guarded secret. This extraordinary lake is the hidden jewel in the crown of the hills of Donegal – a heaven-sent and heaven-set lough complete with a pair of sandy white, tropical-looking beaches. Not to mention a population of gorgeous, pink-fleshed trout. Barry and I hooked one when we were there. The setting proved so hypnotic and unforgettable, the rewards so great, I had to base a story on our experience. Here, the names are different (Aengus being a tribute to W.B. Yeats), but the setting remains, gloriously, the same. What follows is called "Lost Notes" ... and all that's in its pages is true, to the letter. Well, almost ...

2

Lost Notes

Aengus's eyes momentarily widened with alarm. Too wrapped up in childish things to notice that I had steered off the road merely to park, his gaze returned to normal as the wheels of the jeep settled into the soft roadside.

Anyone watching would have thought we were to spend the afternoon in pursuit of fish. Rods in the air, tackle bags on our shoulders, we left the jeep and walked past uniform lines of fertilizer bags puffing out their chests with turf. To our left, a solitary snipe strained its neck and stared at us with beady eye and long straight bill. It knew we were not fishing for fish, but then snipes know everything. I broke eye-contact with the bird and walked on. The wind rose. So did the land. I looked up fearing showers, but the western sky was clear. The hill was steep – steeper for smaller feet.

"How much more?" asked Aengus.

"Not far."

I took his hand as we jumped over a turf-walled trench deep as a grave. Not easy for him, not easy for his father either, plodding over sods that concealed ankle-twisting holes. Bog-cotton waves prettily, beneath it the detritus of ten thousand years opens up. Not easy, rods in hand, bags around neck – balance comes hard, breath comes hard. A stream gurgled to our right. It should not have been to our right. I hoped it was not that stream, the one we should be keeping to our left. Crest of hill confirmed that it was.

A blue-brown lake slid into view as if some unknown god had pushed out a massive, panoramic drawer from the wedge of hill beneath our feet. The drawer contained a mirror sparkling between mountainy folds of heather. My eyes soaked it up. I knew that more than nature was at work here. Magic permeated the air – not the cheap, illusory tricks of gameshow conjurors, but *magick*. I breathed in great lungfuls of it. It seeped, percolated, inebriated – in, through, up, down – filling my senses until I looked at the lake and knew for certain that down in its dark underbelly, something waited.

Loch Natragh, *Loch na Traigh,* Lake of Beaches. Two of them, small and white-sanded, lay at the eastern end. Separated by the merest spit of bogland, they may as well have been miles away. Correct stream, wrong side. To our right an impenetrable gorge; rhododendroned, steep-sided, not for adults much less children.

Below us a marshy bank. Heads bowed predacious-
ly, we slinked to within casting distance. A trout rose in-
vitingly. I ignored the fish and cast out quickly. My red
rose sunk and snagged. I stood up straight and pulled
it free. It snagged again – too many rushes spoiled the
retrieve. Eventually I reeled in my ragged flower and
glared at the rushes. Then I looked at Aengus. He was
waiting to be rigged up. I glanced at the rushes once
more.

"Let's go," I nodded to the western end. "Looks
clearer down there."

He shrugged and sighed a little.

"Best find a good spot before settling down," I added consolingly.

Ours was a circuitous route because we had to
climb another hill; a reed-infested quagmire down by
the shore saw to that. Footholds were difficult, solid-
ity a rare commodity in these parts. I heard Aengus's
ragged breath behind me. It matched his jerky steps.
When I heard him struggle no more I looked and saw it
was because he could not keep up. I waited for him. He
soldiered on gamely, once or twice catching me with
that familiar look which asks why I have to do this, or
more to the point, why he has to do it. I had no answer
to that, so I turned around and marched on.

Ten paces later we reached the top of the hill. With
no warning the ground jumped up a metre. Luckily,
only one of my legs dive-bombed into the bog-hole,
otherwise who knows what depth I may have plumbed.

I pulled my sore, sodden leg out of the morass and smiled ruefully at Aengus. I checked for damage to the rod and reel that fell with me, and looked down at the lake. "Damn," I muttered, cursing my eyesight — rushes were abundant here as well. I should have seen them sooner. Now we faced a hard slog around the far side. "There," I used my wellington as a pointer while I emptied it of water, "about halfway along, there's a place we can cast from."

My steps were prudent now, not just so Aengus could keep up. The terrain was firmer on this side. Huge folds of peat corrugated the land, making walking difficult. Stiffness slithered up my legs. Aengus's breath was still jerky, not entirely from exertion. "Nearly there now," I told him, knowing that his irritability was justified. I promised him milk and chocolate, and told him joyously that the water was free of reeds. Soon we reached the chosen spot. I checked my watch. Forty-five minutes since we stepped from the jeep.

I gave him sustenance, cast my line, and rigged him up. By the time he had made his cast I looked for my bubble float. It was not there. Hope fluttered briefly, then sank. The wind had merely blown the float back to the shoreline.

We cast our bubbles with roses attached — he with three, I with two. When he had finished his refreshments I broke the dreaded news. "It's no use, Aengus, the elements are against us here. Our flowers keep floating back in. Down on those beaches, we'd have no problem. The wind would carry our bait out far." With trepidation I mentioned this for I was fearful that all our setbacks might turn my son against that which I must teach him to do. But the sustenance strengthened him and he reeled in compliantly. Anyway he knew I would not rest until we were in the right place.

Ten more grudging minutes took us to where we should have been in the first place. Now we stood on a little white beach, wind at our backs. I rigged us both up, carnations this time. We had learned that rose petals disintegrated too readily in these conditions. Aengus cast ten metres, I twice that. Length did not matter as the wind carried our flowers out.

We stood on the beach for an hour casting and waiting. Occasionally our bait grew soggy and slipped beneath the surface. Wet carnation, slowly sinking, sometimes works – but not here. We tried different colours: pinks, reds, whites. Nothing took but we were patient, knowing the object of our pursuit was wary, nervous, and utterly unpredictable.

Aengus no longer asked the time. He came under a spell and so did I – the beauty of our surroundings guaranteed it. No trace of man here; no roads, no fences. Only God's own mountain, lake and bog – and man and boy.

Time passed. The sky turned kinder. Clouds chased higher, whiter. No threat of rain now, the wind died as Lake of Beaches became Lake of Glass. Even birdsong ended. A stillness came. It took the wildness from the wilderness and replaced it with an anticipation not conducive to small-talk. The world was pregnant now, and the time was near.

I lay my rod upon the sand, forgetting about the beautiful invitation sinking beneath my float. Nature, *magick*, prayer invaded my spirit. I felt renewed, at one with the universe, at peace with the world. Invisible to Aengus, I shook off the shackles of the world the way a newly-hatched mayfly shakes the water from her wings.

Aengus noticed it first. "Father!" he shouted. "Look!"

Nothing raises the weary spirit, nothing lifts the sinking heart, like the sight and sound of a line going taut. It whipped across the surface like a waterboatman gone mad. It shot out into the middle of the lake, a tiny wake spreading behind it. The rod-tip strained before I could bend to reach. It jerked toward the water before my hand was on it. I grabbed the butt-end just in time, striking quickly. In my fingers that glorious feel, that momentary resistance which signifies but one thing. I reeled in furiously. It fought a little – a living force, an elemental weight. I could sense it thinking about diving back into the darkness. Then it surrendered.

My son stood to the wrong side, net in hand. He has a lot to learn. Wary of losing momentum, and my catch, I decided not to waste time asking him to move to the correct position. "I'm going to beach it," I yelled, knowing it was very close.

The lake exploded two metres out. Something golden broke the surface then disappeared as I pulled hard on the rod and gave the reel one last, mad twirl.

It erupted onto the beach in a fiery cascade of water and sand. There it lay flat, gasping and helpless as a premature baby. Aengus dropped to his knees and huddled over it. Overwhelmed with curiosity, he scanned it up and down with great swoops of his eyes. Unable to take his gaze from it, he asked, "What is it?"

I plucked the carnation from its golden-brown head and watched its azure wings stir a little. I lifted and separated them, blowing lightly. Aengus looked at me this time. With a great gulp of breath he demanded to know.

"Listen," I whispered, and the wings began that frantic, flapping action of the newborn. "Just listen," I whispered again, and he did.

I lifted the golden creature gently from the sand. A tremor ran through it and through me. Aengus and I knelt on the shore, my arms offering a frail, nascent gift to the fading light of day. I stretched up my hands to the sky above, to the red orb of the sun, and to the stars beyond. I bent my head in worship. Aengus instinctively, respectfully, did the same. In the palm of my hand a tiny heart beat.

The weight lifted from my palms and soared into the sky. More than rhythm to its wings now, the creature sang as it flew. There was music. Sacred music. At once new, forever ancient, it filled the mountains with notes of serene beauty. It redefined the space between mountains. Its resonance plumbed the depth of the lake, rebounded below, and echoed back up with a cosmic sonar that broke the surface and made our hearts tremble. Its chords would have felled trees if there had been trees here. A song to die for, it made the setting sun go slowly supernova until its burgeoning orb reached out, finger-pointing us with bright, red rays. The ground trembled beneath us. The lake shimmered as if a giant plectrum had come from somewhere and played the landscape.

All too soon it was gone, free, released. The bearer of trebles to make us tremble, of base notes to touch the hiding places of our minds, had soared so high its notes were lost in cloud. The music faded, the chorus ended, and the sun's glorious rays diminished as the sun itself slipped behind the mountain.

"I know what it is!" Aengus got off his knees and jumped up and down, as if jumping might bring him nearer to the sky and he might hear the lost notes again. "It's a song!" he yelled. "We caught a song!"

Reluctantly from Lough Natragh we trudged. Mindful of bog-holes, mindful of music beyond compare, we made our way to the jeep without mishap. Aengus was full of mountains, lakes and exotic creatures that sing as they fly. In his eyes I saw a look that told me he would spend his life forever in search of that which we released today. For that I was glad, for someone will have to take over from me when I am gone. I knew then that Aengus would be that person, and that is as it should be for he is my son.

But we were back in the realm of humankind with all its frailties and distractions. We drove on tar steam-rolled long ago, past electricity wires long since hung, down to a wider road. There we joined a stream of red tail-lights wandering aimlessly through a concrete environment. We came at last to a driveway. No lakes or mountains here, but at least our home is surrounded by a rampart of broad-leafed trees.

Aengus ran to the figure in the doorway, the story gushing from him. "We caught a song!" he yelled. His mother smiled and patted his head. She took him into the kitchen, heated his supper, and listened patiently while I went over to the yard to put the rods away. By the time his story was over I was bolting the shed. Before I had time to turn I heard the discreet click of the backdoor latch. My wife stepped out. She checked that the latch was secure before walking across the yard. I knew from her look that she had news. I do not know how she knows these things; she always does and is never wrong.

"There was a suicide off the bridge," she whispered. "A young girl."

"When?" I asked, knowing her answer.

"Before sunset." She put her hand on my shoulder and lifted her head. Together we looked up. Clouds had gone and there were stars.

I like to think a new star shone that night, the light of a soul released. But there were too many lights to count. I like to think that the music Aengus and I heard out at the lake was played by Gabriel on his horn, or by the angels on their harps, and that the vocals were the joyous notes of a soul singing in celebration. I silently thanked the stars for giving me the key to unlock these tortured souls, and I put my arm around my wife. We stood there stargazing, secure in the knowledge of our destiny and our task, and secure in the knowledge that there was someone to follow us. Enough for us now to hear him sweetly singing in the kitchen, and enough for him, at his tender age, to think we are merely the fishers of songs.

3

East & South, Young Man

In the 1980s and 1990s, Fermanagh borderposts and British Army checkpoints led us away from Donegal. They beckoned us like spell-casting crones to that alternate space, the real world. A day-job teaching children on the east coast.

The Tempo River roadsign has always been our byword; a magic spell to lift the world, signalling that we were truly in the North. Fermanagh place-names called out to us – incantations, buzzwords, sacred cows grazing across our brains, lowing from passing rhythmic fields: Enniskillen, Lisnarick, Ballinamallard. And then the Pullans, that mountainy time machine rising up from Pettigo. A tourist sign creaked in fuchsia, welcoming us to moorland remote and raw; ruined now by trees tall enough to hide the view, but not big enough to block the ridge of blue mountains stacked high against us: the hills of Donegal, or the sight of John's Point fingering moonlit sea, or the lights of Mountcharles shining out across the bay. Below us, we felt the town draw near – the town where strong hearts beat; the place where we were going, where ghosts and prophets meet.

Except now we were driving back to Dublin, and so doing the journey in reverse. The road up into the Pullans; our eyes and hearts bearing witness to the glummer side of that fuchsia-kissed roadsign, the three words that bid farewell with a plaintive message: "Come Back Soon". Indeed. Then Enniskillen, the Tempo River bridge heralding a turn-off to Maguiresbridge and Lisnaskea, the drumlin-strewn countryside of Cavan, the flat lands of Meath. Finally, Dublin.

Our fishing in Dublin has been infrequent and much too sporadic, to say the least. Perhaps because it's the home patch and too familiar, therefore not alluring. A few boat trips in some of Loughshinny Sea Angling Club's open competitions during the 1990s yielded some results. Plenty of whiting on lug and ragworm, including thirty of them one day, of which Barry took eighteen, in the Hole off Rockabill. A mackerel on feathers from the pier in Skerries where Barry once stroke-hauled a dazed and confused lesser-spotted dogfish that had been discarded and left for dead by local trawlermen. Out in Portrane, a mackerel on feathers from the rocks by the Martello Tower and three pollack, including two for Barry on ledgered lug, from the fishing circle at the west pier in Howth. Not a very impressive list. A list so sparse I'm adding to it our only Wicklow fish –

though he may have been a true blue Dub, because the source of the Glencree River is within casting distance of county Dublin. Later, after the Glencree mingles with the Dargle, its waters again flow within a lobbed Arsley Bomb of the capital. So, who knows, my little Wicklow trout may indeed have been a Dubliner.

The choice was simple: a strenuous hillwalk to the cairn on top of Maulin or a gentle few hours on the Glencree River. No contest. The rest of them gathered in Crone carpark, basecamp for a tough hillwalk to celebrate a fiftieth birthday. I left them to their walk, chuckling to myself with vindictive satisfaction, and sauntered down to a promising pool on a bend in the river where I found peaceful solitude. A light drizzle began to fall, prompting me to move. A sheltered, tree-covered pool lies upstream of the Wicklow Way foot-bridge. Drizzle, now turned to rain, seeped in through the overhanging branches. Wet, slippy, lichen-covered rocks. Rain oozing down mossy trunks and boughs. A wonderful, if tight, spot for casting. More like dangling your fly in the water at your feet and letting it glide down on the current. Not a place to slide sideways and feel cool water seep into a wellington boot and drench a trouser leg. It was worth it though: a small brownie on a Black Pennell on the last cast of a two and a half hour stint. He fought hard and swam for cover, diving and snagging the line on a bunch of underwater roots. I had to wade in and feel my upper legs get wet before I could retrieve enough line to bring him in.

Twenty minutes later, at the reception desk of a local hostel booked for the night as part of the birthday celebrations, I put on my best doleful look, explained my wet trousers, and asked for the room key.

"The rooms won't be ready for hours," said the hostel warden. "However, in your case," her eyes took in my hangdog expression and sopping trouser legs, "I'll make an exception."

Half an hour later, I stood perfumed and coiffured in brand new party clothes, watching the rest of them arrive from the summit of Maulin. They sat around in sweaty, stinking, hiking gear, and asked for their room keys only to be told, "The rooms won't be ready for two hours. The only person I've allowed into his room is the man who fell into the river."

When I heard that, I began to chuckle mischievously again.

Fishing 1, Hillwalking 0.

Next day we drove the short distance to our home in Lusk. I put my rods away as usual, as though Dublin lacked attractive fishing locations, whereas the opposite is the case. The promontory at Dromanagh, between Loughshinny and Rush, is a wonderful spot. The downside is it has only one casting perch. Best get there first, which I did several times on the run from the school bell after class had been dismissed. Imagine a chalkie pointing his face into the breeze to let the cool salt spray and tangy air wipe the white dust from cheeks and mind. Just the place for restoring a soul bruised and battered by the demands of the ever-expanding curriculum of what Pearse called "The Murder Machine". Yet Donegal seemed the natural place to fish in those days, not Dublin. When a rival location emerged to compete for our fishing casts, it turned out to be a most unlikely place.

"Tramore?" I shrieked.

Vague but horrific images of bumper cars, one-armed bandits, waltzers, carousels, rubber ducks, amusement arcades, crane machines, twenty-cent rapids, sand castles, bikers, hucksters, caravans, pedal boats, the *Daily Red Top* in back pockets, mothers of seven screaming at ice cream-demanding children, candy floss, doughnut bars, vinegar-strewn chippers and gougers from inner cities on the loose for their annual week in Ireland's answer to Skegness. All this flashed through my mind in quick succession. "You've got to be joking!" I yelled.

Marie was deadly serious. When she told me that we had bought a mobile home in Tramore, I fainted.

That August I walked from a caravan park in Crobally Lower, on the far eastern side of Tramore, all the way out to the Guillamene, which lies west of the town. "A good place for fishing," said Dixie, the man from whom we had bought the mobile home. I spent some hours casting from one of the fishing spots on the rocks. A gentle swell from the heaving kingdom of the sea lapped the limpets that clung to the rocks at my feet. Out came a pollack so small I nearly missed him on the feather. They all count. If only I knew what I was letting myself in for.

Twenty years of visiting the Guillamene has yielded catches of pollack, mackerel, rockling, herring, lesser-spotted dogfish and foul-hooked sand eel. More than sixty fish in thirty-two visits, at the last count. I've lost track of how many times I've walked away with nothing, but fishing is about a lot more than fish. Take a recent visit, for instance: one unforgettable bright blue October morning a sea otter watched me angle for about half an hour. He had no qualms about coming up close and held no fear of the lone angler on the rocks above his head. Between casts I saw him size me up, dividing his time between swimming around, diving deep beneath the slightest of swells rolling in off the mildest of seas, and treading water watching what the fisherman was at. At one point, reeling in with the otter nowhere to be seen, confident that a fish had already been hooked, there came a tug on the line – a sudden knock similar to the feel of a pollack taking the bait. A pollack-mackerel combo on one cast of my four-hook rig – what a wonderful prospect. So I hauled in, full of hope, only to reel an empty line. Two seconds later, Mr Otter surfaced with a fine mackerel between his teeth. He regarded me an instant, bold as brass, as if to show off his catch and say, "Thanks for serving such a fine dinner, man."

From the rocks at the Guillamene (white-painted shore competition numbers are well faded these days) the sturdy Metal Man stands tall decked out in county colours of blue and white. He is four metres in height and adorns the middle of three sixty-foot towers, finger pointing the way to Waterford harbour entrance. To his left, three miles away on Brownstown Head, two towers. In between Brownstown and the Guillamene, the treacherous rocks and flats of Tramore Bay. In olden days sailors knew to sail beyond the Metal Man, to follow his finger and keep Brownstown Head also to port. Beyond Brownstown, or Brazen Head as it is sometimes known, the fishing village of Dunmore East and safe passage upriver to Waterford. In dark of night with a storm brewing, if you strain your ears and listen hard you might still hear the Metal Man's warning chant:

Keep out, keep out, good ships from me
for I am the rock of misery.

Tramore Bay has claimed more than its share of shipwrecks, the ill-fated troop ship *Sea Horse* being the most well known, going down in 1816 with the loss of 360 lives.

The bay is a haven for all sorts of sea life, and down the years has presented us with eleven varieties of fish: wrasse, whiting, rockling, sprat, mackerel, pollack, sand eel, dogfish, herring and sea trout on all sorts of bait – feathers, spinning lures, ledgered lug and mackerel, floating limpet – not to forget a famous weever fish stroke-hauled while night-casting off the strand to see if our Florida-bound lightweight five-footer could handle a heavy spinner. Barry has taken whiting, sprat and lesser-spotted dogfish here; and for Claire, a rockling down at the pier, a good spot for dipping a little lug to see what knocks on the fisher's door. The main haunt, however, is the Guillamene up near Newtown Cove. Nearby is Newtown Glen where Charles Kickham is said to have written a chapter of *Knocknagow*.

The Guillamene has its faults; a popular spot, unbearably so on an evening tide in July or August, especially at weekends. The rocks become a shooting gallery. Hooks, lead weights, feather lures and spinners fly past ears in a setting as crowded as O'Connell Street at rush hour. Go home when it's like that. Do not be tempted to bother. Return early next morning when the sun slants a silver essence on the sea. Take a hook, wrap foil paper around it. Add on a little strip of bird's feather. Keep your back straight and fly your cast a million miles. Stand on a rocky ledge, salt spume fresh on your cheeks, waves crashing at your feet, gulls diving for fry in the deep blue. Watch fish run: mottled, silver-bellied, in shoals single-minded; darting, diving, turning this way and that, dazzling with their blue-green backs as they swim around. A thousand living torpedoes, metallic, gleaming, their mystic controls set for somewhere deep, somewhere secret that only they would know. But then they surface. The sea boils with sprats and chasing mackerel. Suddenly you are in, the bend of the rod sublime, the smile on your face. Catch a mackerel. Gut it with your sharp knife right there on the rocks. Dip the fish in the sea one last time, bring it home for breakfast.

What better way to start the day? Then spend the afternoon in Waterford or Cheekpoint or Dunmore or Dungarvan or Ardmore or Lismore or, best of all, hill-walk high in the Comeraghs and cast your human eyes on a sea that shimmers all the way from Ballycotton in the west to the Saltees in the east. End the day in Tramore, a town much better than the sum of clichéd images that rattled through my mind when Marie first mentioned coming here. There is a hint of vibrancy about Tramore that stems, not from the constant influx of visitors, but from the town's own people and their fine sense of community and identity, allied with the fantastic natural setting of Tramore Bay. Sure, down-town can be crowded in peak season if the weather is good. The higher part of Tramore remains relatively tourist-free, even in July and August: uphill streets are an Everest too steep for the feet of most holidaymakers. At night, stroll down to Murph's where the pint and the music is always good.

Next day, fish other parts of the bay. Rinnashark and Saleen, for instance – as long as the jet skiers bless you with their absence. On a calm April morning, I watched wild geese fly in V-formation. Birds flocked on sparkling water: oystercatchers, gannets. Sand martins flitted in and out of little caves they had excavated in the walls of sand behind me. Distant spires of Tramore jutted into a clear blue sky. I threw a bass lure into the tidal channel that leads to Saleen and the back strand estuary. Here water flows fast and hard, funnelling in a fusion of ocean currents; strong and irresistible, the force of nature. No place for falling in. My fly rod bent over as though rent in two. The sea exploded a few yards out. Pepé almost wet himself with circle-dancing excitement. He yapped his head off, that curious bark whenever a fish was caught. He back-pawed the sand furiously as I beached a good sea trout, though not very heavy at one pound, nine ounces.

To the east of Tramore Bay juts the prow of Brownstown Head, with a pair of pillars that stand tall like massive artillery guns pointed skyward. I tied a bass lure to the end of the fly rod and jigged it with shimmering temptation off the rocks beyond this pair of warning symbols for errant sailors. There, in the cove between Carraigaunboy and Sruhnaleam, a pollack plunged deep and fought hard before I hauled him up from a stormy sea like a pirate lifting a bar of gold from a sunken treasure chest. Farther east, Barry took a pollack on floated mackerel bait at the mouth of the hidden cove at Ballymacaw, an ideal haven for smugglers and pirates. I brought in a pair of mackerel that fought for all they were worth, again at the spinning end of the fly rod.

From Ballymacaw it's only a couple of miles to Dunmore East. Barry and Claire have taken pollack on ledgered lug, both inside the harbour breakwater or over at the ice plant. Coalfish, with that distinctive white lateral line, and small pouting have given themselves up to lug or ledgered mackerel, these last few to the tune of Pepé's conspicuous and distinctive fish-bark: *arr-ah, arr-ah, arr-ah,* whatever that means in dog language. I once landed twelve mackerel on the rocks southwest of Dunmore harbour. One every three minutes, sometimes a fish on each feather of my three-hooked rig. I started to throw them back and gave up after half an hour. It's no fun when it becomes slaughter. One for sport, two for the pan is enough for any man.

As Donegal has John's Point, Waterford boasts a not-so-secret fishing Shangri-La: Dunabrattin Head, known to locals as Boatstrand, a renowned hotspot for shoals of mackerel and pollack. The headland lies off the coast road, a slippery eel of a road that twists and bends this way and that along the top of the cliffs between Annestown and Bunmahon. Not a road to be hurrying on when out driving. Park the car. Walk out to the old look-out post. Hop over the electric fence and make your way to the water – but tread gingerly, Dunabrattin's rocks are tricky. They say fish are caught here at all states of the tide. I returned empty-handed once out of ten visits. Not bad. Mighty pollack live here, as do baby ones. Catch pollack on floating mackerel. And the mackerel themselves, those glittering creatures so spectacular in colour and sheen some artists devote their lives to specialise in painting them, are no problem to catch. One mid-August day yielded twenty-six in thirty minutes. Just one cast failed to bring up a fish. After half an hour I was so bored I packed away my gear.

Some fishermen thrive on numbers. Good luck to them. That's what floats their boat. Give me an hour, or two or even three, with nothing. Then one little fish to save the day. Give this to me any time, more fun than the relentless reeling in of bucket loads of suicidal fish. Grant me time to take a break from casting, to sit on flat rocks and contemplate the land, the water, the birds that fly and cartwheel in overhead sky. Watch gulls and other birds dive – now *they* know how to fish. Allow my eyes time to examine what floats as flotsam in the ripples at my feet. Let me jettison the jetsam of my life, and get on with taking in the great world that surrounds. The inhaling of things that matter, like smell of salt spray; tang of it in my nostrils of a windy day when I stand thirty feet up to be truly safe from breakers smashing into the rocks beneath, a day when my eyes witnessed but refused to believe what happened next.

A canoeist appeared from left field, paddling hard out of Boatstrand. He turned the corner at Dunabrattin Head, rollercoasting waves like a demented thrillseeker, an escapee from one of the Tramore amusement rides seven or eight miles down the coast. I watched him plough headlong, the sea undulating beneath him like a heaving animal at a rodeo. He disregarded my obvious casting distance, ignoring the lone fisherman totally. My eyes jumped again. Like buses, another canoeist came along, also paddling hard out of Boatstrand. This second canoe promptly capsized, dumping its owner into the raging water of an utterly capricious sea. The first guy, who had paddled away towards the horseshoe cove at Kilmurrin and now had his back to me, had no idea that his buddy had gone over. I yelled a warning, bursting my lungs to beat the howling wind. He heard and turned to see me point at his distressed companion.

The first canoeist paddled like the cartoon clapppers back to his friend's overturned canoe. It soon became clear that the canoeist in the water was incapable of clambering aboard his craft, which his companion had now uprighted. For minutes I watched him try to haul himself up only to fall back every time. His friend tried to help him but with no success. He bobbed up and down, helpless, a cork floating in stormy water. I reached for my phone, ready to dial 999 and call the coast guard, but the fringe of this remote headland proved to be beyond mobile phone reception. Not even a sprat of a signal.

Luckily for him, the stricken canoeist managed to hold on to the stern of his own canoe. His friend tied the bow of the empty canoe to his stern, and paddled furiously through the waves to safety. It was like watching a loco with two carriages ride on a switch-back mountain railroad. Up and down, up and down. I shook my head. The sea does not discriminate. The sea takes all sorts of victims, hero and idiot alike. I know which category those two were in.

Sometimes, the mongrel mind of the fisher-writer goes to a dark place. Perhaps prompted by an experience like that described above, or maybe after seeing the amount of litter discarded by other anglers. Plastic bags, lure wrappings, beer cans, loose lines and poisonous lead weights deadly for birdlife, all these things are scattered everywhere. Left behind by careless anglers who, given what they are engaged in, ought to be the first people to have respect for the environment and the creatures that dwell in it. The Guillamene is a particular black spot in this regard, but it is subject to more angler traffic than any other location I know.

Sometimes the landscapes and seascapes darken with cloud or rain or evening gloom, or with despondency bred of lack of fish – or perhaps something else is at work, trawling the depths of the fisher-writer's mind. An imagination overfed on dark tales can take something simple, a fishing diary, for instance, and turn it into an unpleasant piece, nasty even; dark pages that plumb the deepest, gloomiest depths of the inner sea. The story that follows, called *The Fishing Log* is, I am happy to say, untrue. It is merely the product of one such avid, rabid and, thankfully, overfertile imagination. I make no apologies for repeating, in the following story, fishing information already given, or to be provided in later chapters of this book.

4

The Fishing Log

January 1 – St Pete's Beach, Florida. Getting children to talk is like fly fishing. Float it right and they will rise. On Merry Pier, not far from the Colonial Gateway Hotel, a pair of mangrove snappers plus a little red grouper for Raymond on bait lent to us by a kind local who fished from a deck-chair while listening to a ballgame on his radio, beer bottle in one hand, rod in the other. Talk about laid-back. Raymond and I did not chat about serious things today – we were on our holidays, after all. Evonne and Amy left us to our day's fishing; they spent the afternoon at the hotel pool.

January 5 – From the walkway under John's Pass Bridge in Madeira Beach, Raymond and I shared six sea-cats, one of which had spines that left a very sore hand. The girls again stayed at the hotel. Our last day here. Tomorrow we fly back to cold, wet rain.

March 1 – At last, trout season opening day. After an hour casting into a bitter northwesterly out at Valley Bridge, a small rainbow (an escapee from the local fish-farm) came to the worm. Gave it another hour. Freezing hands despite gloves and deep pockets. A day for the hip-flask. Big change from Florida. Great to be back in sacred, spiritual places where, despite chills and damp, ghosts of history abound, trout rise, and sons and daughters speak.

March 8 – Our second day in a row fishing the Dowber River. Two tiddler brownies for Amy, including one caught on a bubble-float abandoned overnight. "My first river fish!" she exclaimed. Raymond was jealous. A greedy perch on his Heather Moth placated him. We chatted about fishing, of course, before I floated my fly-questions about what really mattered: school, friends, problems. They took the bait: important to get them talking, to open up, to communicate. Arrived home to a warm dinner. Evonne was glad I had taken the kids. Gave her the afternoon to herself.

March 17 – After four hours' angling, a fine St Patrick's Day trout (two pounds, three ounces) on the twilight rise by the far bank at Miller's Lake. The lads from work were well oiled by the time I joined them afterwards in the pub.

March 28 – Spinning off the pier with Raymond. His first day with the shiny new five-foot rod; my present for his ninth birthday. Along came two tourists, Germans by the sound of them. Barely room for four rods. Hooks and lead weights whizzed past us. Ten minutes later one of the tourists guffawed, "Three of us here and no fish! Well," he glanced sarcastically at my son, "three and a half, actually!" A quarter of an hour later the half landed the only catch of the evening – a joy to see the perplexed look on the tourists' faces. Raymond was thrilled. His first pollack. He sat beaming in the front seat all the way home.

April 15 – River Belent. Solitude, as pure as only fishing can bring. Alone, except for a moorhen. The river a moving script, two capital Vs written in watery ink. One, the wake left by the moorhen, the other the trace of my Green Peter as I jerked the fly along the surface. I studied these twin hieroglyphs of man and waterfowl. Our shared impulses instinctive, primal, intent on the same pursuit, one unified goal: to extract what secrets the river holds. I felt in consort with the moorhen as it rounded the river bend. If reincarnation does exist, we could do worse than return as a moorhen, or perhaps a swan.

April 26 – At the waterworks weir on a day made for fishing in bare feet. Raymond caught a fingerling brownie on a Wickham's Fancy and a small perch on the black and silver salmon fly. Those midges! We stopped for ice cream on the way home, after a few pints at the Horse & Wagon.

May 11 – The sandy shore opposite the estuary. Marram grasses tall as sentries on dunetops this calm morning. Razorbills flock on sparkling water and wild geese fly in clear blue sky. A good sea trout (five pounds, twelve ounces) rose to a bass lure. Put up a decent fight, too. No net so had to beach him. We feasted on him for days. A wild sea trout beats a farmed salmon any day. Even Amy had a few mouthfuls. Like most ten-year-olds she's picky about fish, though she enjoyed catching those brownies out in the valley. Her brother Raymond will not eat fish flesh though he's keen on hooking it. Evonne was impressed by my catch and said so. Her first compliment of the year: overdue and all the more welcome for that. Man-the-hunter still registers for something in her scheme of things. God knows she's distant enough these days.

May 20 – River Belent. Four dace from a stick-float with trotted maggot upstream of the railway bridge. Such a beautiful day. Reflections of trees in the water indistinguishable from real ones on land, except for being upside down. Like fishing in a Constable painting, or perhaps a Turner.

May 26 – Off the rocks near the beach: a pollack on feathers – a poor return for two hours. High tackle attrition rate; never noticed that here before. Hooks and weights kept snagging. Will have to re-stock in the tackle shop tomorrow. Saw a kayak capsize before my eyes in a choppy swell. No phone reception out here to ring the coast guard but he righted himself, lucky for him. Broke an old reel on my new ten-foot rod, and the rod on its first day out! Transferred a small reel from my six-footer and used a sprat lure to catch a mackerel. Then another one came along. Never caught mackerel shore-fishing in May before. They're very early this year. Climate change?

June 2 – Not a bite all day. Must be Evonne souring the water with her fish-repellent thoughts. She's spending more and more time with that drama group, whatever the attraction is. She treats me much the same way the fish are right now: pretending I don't exist.

June 10 – From Louis Harfar's thirty-six footer on the drift near Sovereign Rocks: Raymond landed and counted every one of seventy-three mackerel, no less. Joy shone like sea spray on his face. Definitely two fish-ermen in our family now.

June 16 – Bloomsday picnic at Idir Lake. Just me and the children. Evonne and I share little these days, not even quality time with Amy and Raymond. They angled for stickleback using worms at the end of the five- and six-footers and had great fun watching golden flashes; little bellies turning as the fish tried to swallow the gigantic worm. At one stage we had three sticklebacks in our jar, just like my own childhood days. I didn't angle except to extract a wine-fish – a bottle of Shiraz I'd put in the water for cooling as soon as we arrived lakeside.

June 22 – The rocks off End Point. Raymond caught a lesser-spotted dogfish on a three-pronged hook too deep to extract. The fish writhed and vomited to a slow death in my hands. My son's face clouded over with the harshest of summer squalls. I will never forget the shadow of shock and horror in his eyes – his heart and soul plummeting to the depths. He looked at me accusingly as though I had personally introduced him to a world of suffering, depravity, cruelty and pain – I had, in a way. I blame myself, but we cannot keep our children innocent forever. Back home, when he told his mother what had happened, Evonne gave me a look as if I were my children's gateway to a fallen world.

July 3 – From the back seat of Jim Baker's canoe: two mackerel on cod feathers. One jigged out by Rock Island, the other trolled near the beach by the cove. I forgot to bring a priest. Jim obligingly pulled ashore near the island to allow me pick up a suitable stone.

July 10 – Downstream from the Old Road Bridge in a filthy stretch of water. Waded out under the trees. It takes great accuracy to thread a fly through rapids caused by abandoned shopping trolleys, rusty beer cans and busted bikes. A twelve ounce brown trout on a Greenwell's Glory – only bite in two and a half hours though they were rising. Retrieved a bubble-float and a team of attached flies snagged high in branches from a previous visit. Nice. On my own today despite the summer holidays. Ever since that imbecilic, anti-everything, so-PC teacher tut-tutted one of his pupils for writing a story about the joy of fishing, Raymond keeps making excuses for not coming with me. "Carl says he's calling over." "There's a gang of us going to town." "Naw, Dad, I want to stay in." At least the fool won't be teaching Raymond in September when my son starts in a new class.

July 16 – Off the flat rocks near Hangman's Bay: a rare catch, a shimmering herring plucked from a sun-kissed wave on a stormy sea. Went night-fishing that dusk on the Edris. Darkness descended, transporting me to another world. No one left on Earth, no one in existence, not one survivor in the entire length and width of the galaxy. Looked up at stars and planets. Wispy white shroud of the Milky Way sparkled in universal silence except for the murmur of moving water, the rustle of small creatures in the bushes. Reflections of stars glistened in the depths of dark shallows. Suddenly, a dorsal fin splashed in silver water, a fleeting tug on my line ...

July 23 – High up beyond Mountain View, in among the wind turbines, a small brownie came to a Blue Dun. My guidebook describes this lake as 'remote, peaceful and very beautiful' – which, sadly, is no longer the case. That book was written before the turbines came. Those eerie monstrosities loom overhead, destroying the countryside.

August 2 – The Algarve on a holiday. Evonne says it's a family week. No "skiving off", as she put it, "to fish on your own". As a compromise we joined a tourist party on a twelve-rod catamaran for a spot of reef-fishing. It wasn't a bad catch for two of us (Evonne and Amy could not be bothered): three small saddled sea-bream and a bream I could not identify (note: yellow lateral lines, large pectorals, small dorsal), plus a pair of fan-eca – all caught on ledgered cockle. Raymond hauled in one of the bream. He looked happy but I could tell the buzz was gone from his face. No longer a natural fisherman. Joining in just to please Dad. I wish Evonne would do the same. Christ, I needed a few beers that week confined with her.

August 12 – Back to routine Irish summer: cloud and rain. Off the promontory southwest of the inlet: thirty mackerel in ten minutes. At least one on each cast, of-

ten a fish on every feather. This kind of angling bores
me. Apart from a few to eat I'm strictly a catch-and-
release man. I don't know how match-fishermen do it
with their keep-nets bulging. Give me two hours with
nothing and then one good catch rather than this wea-
risome slaughter. Threw back most of them. A quarter
of an hour after setting up I had four in my bag for the
pan and my rod dismantled. It's amazing the amount
of drama group rehearsals Evonne is going to. She certainly is acting funny these days.

August 27 – A family picnic on the shores of Rock Lake.
Amy and Raymond cast out floats. Their fishing was
perfunctory though Raymond hooked a good rudd on
a sweetcorn bait. I fished for pike. No luck today. She's
been talking to them about me, I know it. My only haul
was the wine-fish.

"Here we are," I smiled. "Catch of the day."

Evonne glared at the bottle. "That joke's wearing a
bit thin." Her face was set in brimstone.

August 30 – Of all things, a sand-eel foul-hooked on a
feather-rig at ebb-tide near the ice plant in the harbour.

September 1 – "It's time we had a talk," said my wife.
Just when I was at the door, rod in hand, ready to fish
the Roxlent!

September 9 – Above the second falls upstream of the cattle-grid bridge on the Argish River, after more than three hours with worm, cheese and fly rod, at last, to the worm – a minnow. I spent the rest of the day in Reynard's Pub before returning home. They were all gone to bed. Evonne was asleep. Not that it mattered. She turned off her tap years ago.

September 22 – A stray pouting snagged on my feather-rig while fishing in the rain waiting to meet Tom Carroll for a pint – who never showed up. With the coming of the equinox, gales blew through me whenever I fished. Mists of autumn descended, enveloping like a deadly mesh of weighted net falling all around, closing in, tightening. She told her lawyer I was too self-centred, obsessed, a dreamer too fond of the drink. These things may be true, but at least I'm not the one who cheated.

September 30 – Game-fishing season closed today. Have to make-do with sea and coarse-angling from now on. I've been slipping up: I've neglected to update my log. Here's some fishing info I left out – I'll fill in more details later if I remember them:

October 7 – A coalie hauled from a roiling sea using a bass lure on the fly rod. Later, a little south of the usual place, a wrasse on a cocktail of lug and ragworm.

October 23 – Down between the pier and slip, in among the trawlers, stroke-hauled a dazed tope discarded from one of the deep-sea boats. Weighed him (seven-and-a-half pounds). I miss not having Amy and Raymond by my side on days like this. There's so much I could get them to talk about, watching the water.

October 31 – A specimen Halloween pike (twenty pounds, eleven ounces) at Rock Lake. Fish of the Year.

November 20 – Half a dozen roach on sweetcorn out at the reservoir. Thank God for work. The lads at the factory keep me going.

December 13 – Abbot River. An illegal half-pound brownie on the second cast above the bypass bridge on the northern road. Then nothing.

December 21 – Switched to a sprat lure after losing three rigs in four casts. No luck. I fished in a vacuum. My rod dangled through a wormhole into nebulous depths at the far end of an alien universe. I sat waiting for something, anything. Bites were those of phantom snappers. Vibrations of rod and line, oscillations in my floats, all caused by wind, tides and other natural phenomena.

December 25 – It's like fishing in Main Street here on the pier. So many happy families out strolling; walking off carbs or working up appetites, pointing their fingers and raising their eyebrows at a lone fisherman out trying his luck on Christmas Day. Had my two hours with Amy and Raymond this morning. Gave them their presents. "For God's sake make it something other than fishing gear!" she snapped over the phone when I rang to make visiting arrangements. She had decided, without consultation, to take them to her mother's for Christmas dinner. Typical. I gave my children game-consoles (with a virtual fishing game included in the packages).

December 28 – All day my hooks have snagged on weed and rock. It's getting dark. Stars, moon and planets no longer reflect in the water, which looks murky, deep and bottomless. Before we split, I searched Evonne's eyes for reconciliation. She would not allow me back in. My suspicions about that drama group had been well founded: she had a new leading man. I stare now at the womb-like comfort of the sea. I must stop getting so personal; this is meant to be a fishing log. I wish I had someone to confide in, to talk to about this.

December 31 – Jim Baker is in Spain for the New Year. No need to ask him if I can borrow his canoe. I know the brick that hides the spare key to his shed. The sea is flat calm, not an ounce of wind, like the night the *Titanic* sank, and just as numbingly cold. My lure falls into the dark. I force myself to keep on trying. Sooner or later something will bite. I need to retrieve, cast out again, re-ignite my hopes with one last fish. I promised myself to be a good separated father for Amy and Raymond, to support them, to see them as often as she allows, as the family court will allow.

Sounds of chimes and cheers drift from the shore. Fireworks split the sky. I put my stern to midnight jollity and leave them to their Burns' song, their kisses and false bonhomie. After all, they can't see me now. I reel in, no longer interested in fishing, and let the sea take me.

I drift on an ebbing tide and paddle out more and more until my arms begin to ache. The swell is rising. I slip my paddle over the side, a silent offering to Neptune that he may welcome me with open arms. I hope Jim will forgive me for wrecking his canoe. I glance astern. House lights flitter like specks on the horizon. I keep looking over my shoulder, wondering whose house Amy and Raymond are in at this moment, and whether or not she allowed them stay up for the ringing of New Year bells.

5

Locations Exotic & Not Exotic

A blond dude wore white chinos, dark blue shirt and cool, chino-matching, sun hat. He sat fishing two rods from a deckchair on the wharf at Merry Pier in Pass-a-Grille. His pair of thirteen-footers hovered over fish-rich waters, bending frequently under the pull of another successful cast. His transistor radio rested on the wooden planks of the pier, tuned to a baseball match. We watched him listen to the game, catch monsters, and knock back cans of beer.

Thirty feet away at the other end of the wooden planks, Barry and I took turns with the lightweight five-footer we had brought with us on our holidays. Irish spinning lures yielded nothing. Pelicans perched on the bulwarks of the wharf eyed us stoically. I believe they were laughing. The baseball fan took pity on a pair of tourists who clearly had no clue how to fish his patch. He walked over and handed us some mackerel bait. We copied his ledgering technique and reeled in three mangrove snappers from around the wharf, including one for Barry.

Somewhere in among watching distant lightning strikes roll around like drunks brawling along the horizon to Tampa, and listening to baseball chatter waft on warm evening breeze, there came a break in the sports coverage. The word "Ireland" leaped like a giant marlin across the pier at me. That is, I thought I had heard mention of Ireland. I looked at Barry. We shrugged our shoulders and fished on. At the end of our session I asked the friendly dude to photograph one of our snappers. He strolled over with that look on his face – it was written in his eyes: "Are you serious? A trophy-photograph of you holding a sprat?" He obliged. It was our first American fish. Welcome to Florida.

That night, a few miles down the road in the Colonial Gateway Hotel, we tuned the television to a news channel and discovered why Ireland had been mentioned in a news bulletin on an American radio station. It had been the day of the Omagh bombing.

Two days later, from the walkway under John's Pass Bridge at Madeira Beach, Barry lifted another mangrove snapper on ledgered squid we'd bought from a tackle shop nearby. We also shared six sea cats, and rather sharp dorsal spines. One of the cats left me with a very sore hand. A hard, sharp spine pierced right up into that soft slab of flesh between index finger and thumb. Bloodshed. I felt faint and had to sit on the walkway steps for a few minutes. I wrapped my wound in a handkerchief. Soon, normal service resumed and I continued fishing. All was well with the world until we strolled up the walkway to the nearest place of refuge where I could wash my wound – the welcoming lights of a large wharfside bar/restaurant.

"Just need to run my hand under a tap – sorry, faucet." I said to the staff as I strolled in, restrooms in my sights.

"I'm sorry, sir. We cannot let you do that."

My mouth fell open like a fish's. "Why not?" I continued a crab-like walk to the restroom.

The bouncer moved to block me. "Sir, please leave."

"But I'm a tourist. I'm here on holiday ... vacation. I cut myself fishing."

"I don't care where you're from, sir. Or what you were doing. You're not coming in here."

The bouncer was not alone. Back-up arrived in the form of a bartender eyeing me suspiciously.

The stranger in their midst may have looked wind-blown; he may have clutched a bloodied handkerchief, but he was not Freddy Krueger from *Nightmare on Elm Street*.

"Ok," I said. "I'll just take one of these."

"No, you will not, sir."

The bartender moved to protect his stash of paper serviettes stacked neatly on the bar counter near the door. I lunged for a successful catch of a few sheets and made my way out. No point in trying to persuade this pair of gorillas, too set in silvertop ways. I cast in their direction some not-so-nice mutterings about rigid US psyche and choice sarky remarks about American hospitality. What really annoyed me was the name of the premises. It was called *The Fisherman's Friend*.

A couple of days later we parked our hired green Plymouth opposite Merry Pier. We were back in Pass-a-Grille, all four of us eager for a charter fishing trip. There was no sign of the cool dude with the chinos, dark blue shirt and sun hat, sitting on the wharf. What met us instead was a grumpy looking character – overweight, receding hair, sweat-faced – sitting behind a desk in the charter company office. My assumption that he was the boss turned out to be correct. First thing he did was tell me to walk back out to the road and turn the Plymouth around. "Your car has to point a certain way, depending on the side you park."

He was not kidding. I turned the car around without once shaking my head.

On a boat twenty miles out in the Gulf of Mexico, I caught two grey snappers and a red grouper. Barry hauled in two greys, two reds and one amazing triggerfish. A crewman explained how the creature known as triggerfish got its name. "See," he pointed at the dorsal fin and demonstrated with forefinger on fish, "you can cock and uncock the trigger on its back."

Claire took two greys and two reds. Marie lifted four greys plus a pair of reds. A haul of eighteen. A good day's fishing for the four of us. A can was handed around for tips as we neared the wharf. Not a good idea to refuse to tip the crew while you're still on board – with the boat, technically, at sea.

About forty-eight hours later, off Pinellas Bayway Bridge on the way to St Pete's, Barry took our farewell American fish – a sea cat on ledgered squid. We also looked down on the surreal sight of a huge ray sailing underwater like a cloaked and floating alien. Overhead, what looked like Air Force One escorted by four jets. Perhaps it was President Clinton on his way to an appointment with Monica.

On August 22 we checked out of our hotel and drove up the freeway. A three hour drive to just north of Orlando. We were ready to board a ten-hour flight from Sanford back to Ireland. The airport check-in lady told me my five-footer would have to go below in the cargo hold. "Why?" I asked.

"Because it is classified as a weapon."

How could she have known that Barry and I had used that rod to lethal effect when, nightcasting one warm Summer's night on Tramore beach, testing out the rod before deciding to bring it with us to America, we had stroke-hauled a weever fish, of all things, out of a moonlit sea? So rather than use it to ill effect in the cabin, the rod had to be stored below. More US bullshit, I reckoned. If only we knew how fast the world was changing.

Six years on, an exclusive verandah hotel – guests in crisp, open-necked shirts and clean-cut pants. Iced towels handed out by pretty maids to men and women lying on poolside loungers. They lay like seals, though some were walruses, comatosed by the heat of the sun. We were just around the corner from Grand Baie. My feet dangled off the hotel dock. I watched aghast as a speedboat pulled in and tied up a few yards from me. It carried in its bowels two men and two women clearly the worse from a day of tearing around the Indian Ocean ripping up the water on a diet of speed and *Green Island Gold*. The tranquil gardens of Pamplemousses were not for them. Noise is something not needed when fishing. They did not stay long. Soon they untied and went their merry way, eager for more reef busting. Scared away the fish from all around Mauritius, though.

Having caught nothing, I approached Imran, a boatman who made his living by hanging around the shoreline at the edge of the hotel grounds hoping to catch tourists. We arranged for three hours next morning.

A couple of hundred yards off Pointe Eglise, Imran threw in bait – a grubby mixture of squid and bread. The sea boiled over with fish. I'd never seen anything like it. A miniature typhoon was blowing just under the surface and all around the hull of Imran's motorised rowboat. It was a crazy, beatific scene. Cap Malheureux away to port, a headland haunted with beauty. To our stern, the majestic island of Coin De Mire jutted out of the sea like a prop from *Lost Worlds*. The nasal undertow of waves breaking on distant reefs; ocean fizzing like fishy champagne beneath us. Clear blue sea and sky around and above us. The azureness of it all was mind blowing; the salty tang of Indian Ocean better than wind-in-the-hair from a Ferrari.

Fish were frenzied. They threw themselves at fistfuls of bait sprayed over the side by the giant hands of Imran. It took a long time for fishy nostrils to detect the bread on the end of my two-hook rig. When they did, a pair of what Imran pronounced, in his heavily French-influenced way, as *pretaire* took at the same time. To say I hauled in two fish would be an overstatement. I whipped aboard a pair of feathers. They resembled a cross between two small Mediterranean bream and a couple of angel fish, complete with vertical stripes. I later identified them, appropriately on account of the stripes, as sergeant-major fish. Sheepishly, I asked Imran for a trophy-photo. He obliged without batting an eyelid. A short while later he indicated it was time for going in, though we had been out only an hour and a half. Imran had had enough.

One handy thing about a golf bag, apart from the obvious, is that it's made for transporting weapons, as imagined by American airline check-in staff – five-foot rods, for instance. There were twelve of us on that plane. In golfing terms, three fourballs. Five days of golf, one day off. Or, five days golf, one day fishing.

Soon after arriving in our Spanish hotel I informed Maurice, friend and roommate for that trip, that the lid had come loose on a box of maggots I had brought with me from Ireland as bait.

"Some maggots have escaped in the confines of our hotel room," I said, adding not to worry if he found any crawling around on his bed that night. "Maggots are essentially harmless creatures," I assured him.

Maurice looked at me sideways. For a moment I thought he believed me, which gave cause for a laugh, but he and the other ten golfers laughed side-splittingly at me a few days later after I had booked an inshore reef-fishing trip in a booking office down by the marina. It turned out that this sea trip I had pencilled in for our non-golfing day coincided with the one morning in the year when Spanish fishermen decided to take industrial action and flex their muscles by blockading all ports, including that of Fuengirola. So, no charter trip.

Nothing for it but to tramp down to the hotel kitchen and beg for bait before waddling disconsolately down to the shoreline, five-footer in one hand, bait in the other; hope, as always, in the heart. That was Wednesday, non-golfing day. On the Saturday morning, though, I was ready. Knowing the flight home was not until late in the day I pilfered bait at the hotel breakfast.

Usually the three fourballs went to Portugal every October. To put it more accurately, they went to Vilamoura. Portugal and Vilamoura are two separate entities. Though connected physically, they should never be mixed up. Vilamoura stands jowl to shoulder with a town called Quarteira. One is an old town that reeks of fish, the other a new playground smelling of money. Twin towns together, they stand like partners in an illicit sex act. One a rich man, bespoke, the overseas owner. The other looks dishevelled, a fisherman hobo bending over. Quarteira *is* Portuguese, but Vilamoura remains an artificial construct, the *ingénue* of offshore exiles peddling money on the shores of the Algarve. A plaything project built by tax avoiders, anything in designer-built Vilamoura that resembles anything Portuguese is coincidental and non-intentional. This town is sanitised, internationalised, plagiarised. It makes you long for frosts, clouds, rain, radiators, the nourishment of harsh seasons beneath skies dark and Celtic. Why return so often? The mitigating circumstance and saving grace being the pleasure and companionship of the group of golfers I was with.

You can tell you're in Vilamoura because men wander around the marina in groups of four, eight, twelve, sixteen. They wear smart casual trousers. Diamond-patterned pullovers dangle on their shoulders. Most of them sport snazzy yellow socks. The marina is full of Karaoke joints, rip-off restaurants, tacky hotels with keyboard crooners whose aim in life is to send lounge bar residents to sleep with cranked out dirges; over-priced wine bars, nightclubs, shops that target tourist wallets, Irish pubs, and yachts. Lots of yachts – most of them in hock to the banks.

They should block up the harbour to all except trawlers; plant fruit trees in floors of Irish pubs; open fish markets in the casino and nightclubs; collect those bright diamond sweaters and smart casual trousers and hang them on tennis rackets from rigging of cruisers. Make a flag for the fleet of bright yellow socks and sail them all out to the Pillars of Hercules. There the speculators and developers should be weighed down with prawns in their pockets and sucked beneath waves of scorn to the deeps where ghosts of pirates reside – an unsuitable place for investment.

While some of the surrounding estuaries and coastal areas of Vilamoura have been turned into golf courses, most of which are, admittedly, rather good, they ought to give some of it back to the birds, the estuaries, the beaches and turn *some* of the golf courses into meadows for goats and for sheep – and as for the town of Vilamoura itself, down from the mountains bring fine swarthy men of Quarteira to clear it all out and begin again.

The fishing is not great, either. Too often, October winds and tides whistle and splash up and down the southern Portuguese and Spanish coasts all the way from Cape St Vincent in the west to the Straits of Gibraltar in the east. The inclemency of this wind and tide prevents charter boats setting out, even for inshore angling. If the sea is calm, the moment has to be seized. I once hitched a ride on a twelve-rod catamaran to a reef a mile or so off Vale do Lobo – a magnet for all sorts of fish. For my effort I collected two small sea bream and a pair of faneca (a type of pouting), all on ledgered cockle. If stuck onshore in Vilamoura, options are rather limited: set up a series of tiny hooks (size 14 or smaller) on a ledgered rig. Two years after the Spanish trip, a six-hook rig brought in three saddled bream on bread (they prefer hotel white to hotel brown) off the town's east breakwater wharf.

The fishing in the Med felt much better that year we went to Spain. Seven fish in four varieties: sea bream, saddled bream, rock blennies, and a silver-bullet mullet blessed with a sharp yellow lateral line. All caught on the seaward side of the breakwater between Fuengirola marina and the sea, or in the marina itself.

Alan, golfing organiser for our tenth October trip, persuaded the group to try elsewhere in Portugal. We ended up in Estoril, nestled delightfully between the resort of Cascais and the vibrancy of Lisbon. A location that felt like heaven – the real Portugal, at last. Plenty of tourists but, more importantly, foreign interlopers like us got drowned out by the great and friendly numbers of holidaying Portuguese. This is where the natives go, and they ought to know the best spots.

Cascais has tourist bars and English pubs. We avoided them, having learned from misspent afternoons in Vilamoura that English pubs in Portugal are full of tattooed loudmouths, bursting out of Union Jack shorts, or elderly ex-pat couples who laugh too long and too loudly at little or nothing. They sup their drinks slowly, counting down passing afternoons in measured sips. Each hoot of laughter forced, contrived, dog-rough. A retirement in Hell. Their highlight of getting through the day witnessed by mute strangers who couldn't get out of the bar quickly enough.

The non-golfing day in Estoril yielded no fish: tide running wrong. Very little life in the rod. After a couple of hours my pal (and new roommate) Dominic spotted me while swimming off the nearby beach. After his swim he strolled out to to the end of Tamariz Pier, situated just opposite the railway station close to our hotel. Time to reel in and settle ourselves down to a nice lunch in a nearby beach café. Grilled Portuguese sardines, perhaps with shellfish – or maybe a *cozido* – or did we have a burger with an egg on top?

Saturday, though, was a late flight day – and an eked-out hour and a half in the same spot sitting in the sun at Tamariz, feet dangled over the side, watching the world go by. Amazing what you observe, in sea, on land, when you sit rod in hand – the posturing, the ogling; the secret yearnings of men and women who think they are unobserved. The eyes of the fisherman see everything from behind a dark pair of shades.

After an hour a large mullet gobbled the hook, but I was sitting down on the pier edge, too hung over, too slow to react, to bring him up correctly. I nearly fell off the pier with the shock of his pull. He executed a figure-of-eight on the surface and waved cheerio with his fins, headed for the deep. Time to check the watch.

Time to go. I raised my rig to the surface: still two bits of hotel bap on a couple of hooks. I stood wearily – warily, nearly falling in again – bobbing the rod up and down, thinking, why did it take us ten years of coming to Portugal to discover that the hotel chain we stay in does a nice line in poached eggs on toast at breakfast – all we had to do was ask? I reeled in for the last time that trip, and felt a wobble.

I unhooked a small fish. One of those compulsory dwarf Iberian sea breams, naturally. A nice end to a good golfing week in the real Portugal, the harbinger of yet another sea bream to come when, the following October, we returned to the Lisbon area. Our golfing trip that year was notable for torrential rainfall most of the rest day – the sacred fishing day. Wearing full golf wet-gear, as well as two pairs of socks, proved not enough to keep the rain out. Holding a rod with a four-hook rig in one hand and umbrella in the other is not a good idea, especially when the topmost hook snags in the brolly and the bottommost barb does its best to dig into your finger when trying to release the brolly.

I walked a wet and winding road from the hotel to *Boca do Inferno*, a renowned fishing spot a mile to the west of Cascais. A sniffy local looked down his nose at my holiday five-footer and wagged his finger as if to say, *Não Senhor*. One look at the *Inferno* proved how right he was. Heavy tackle, strong line and serious weights were needed to deal with those breakers. I trudged with tail between legs back into town to the

Clube Naval de Cascais – the sailing club where, of course, fishing is not allowed. Making myself as inconspicuous as possible – hard to do when wearing glistening bright blue wet-gear and carrying a large red and white golf umbrella – I ignored the *Pesca Proibida* signs and slinked between two boat huts, a spot that yielded some shelter from toffee-nosed club members and teeming rain. With brolly wedged overhead between the huts, I fished for an hour using exclusively hotel white. Twenty minutes in, there came a welcome knock on the line as the sea surrendered the best ever miniature fish of all my Portuguese trips. Suddenly, the sky cleared, the sun shone – well, nearly. I hauled him in. I regret not digging through layers of wet-gear to extract my mobile phone and take a photo of that saddled bream, a fine specimen.

Determined not to be rained on again, we spread twelve pairs of wings deeper south the following year – and went on our trip a month earlier.

That September saw the group spend more than a week (thanks to Aer Lingus cancelling the return flight) in the Canaries. Part of the package consisted of a two-day trip to La Gomera Island. Our stay in a cliff-top hotel proved memorable not only for fine swimming pools, great food and first class facilities, but because access to the shoreline lay via a lift-shaft drilled deep through solid cliff rock to a tunnel (not for the claustrophobic) leading to a rocky beach. Entry to the lift was granted through the use of a hotel keycard – likewise for the journey back up. The lift-shaft and tunnel experience turned out to be something from a James Bond movie. How to follow such a spectacular descent to the beaches and village beneath the hotel? Consider spending three hours of your brief life on this Earth in the farthest of faraway places perched on the edge of an isolated pier facing a sleepy village, a sparsely populated beach nearby, a vista of your fabulous hotel sitting atop outstanding cliffs; consider blue skies above your head framed by an Olympus Mons mountain backdrop; a cooling breeze to dampen down the heat that might scorch your ardour; plenty of strong suntan lotion on face and arms and legs; the shade of a pier wall to keep your supply of bottled water from overheating; a straw hat to prevent your head combusting in noonday sun as it surely would in a setting of such dramatic beauty; and strong shades to filter light so sharp it would cut your eyeballs in two. Not to mention water so crystal clear that not only is the ocean floor visible, you also see schools of fish shoaling this way and that beneath your dangling feet; water so transparent you view the fish dashing about when the hook is set and the fish is being played; water so clear you cannot tell, exactly, when the fish is out of the sea because water and air seem melded into one divine element.

Exotic, volcanic, La Gomera yielded the best ever fishing return on the golfing rest day: eight fish comprising five varieties – including three species new to the business end of the rod. The catch consisted of a trio of sardines, a pair of ornate wrasse, a super little sharp-nose puffer, one sea bream and a large blue-grey member of the wrasse family whose exact species I have yet to identify. This time my camera was at the ready so I have a photographic record of all five types, and will identify the mysterious wrasse in time.

That late flight back on the final day gave a second opportunity to fish near our base hotel on Tenerife. A hot and humid two-hour stint on breakwater rocks at the entrance to San Miguel Marina yielded one catch, a brilliantly coloured ornate wrasse; an aptly named species, a bright fish with fluorescent green-brown stripes running the length of its streamlined body and a wonderful blue luminescence around snout and gills – a fish that almost, though not quite, made up for all the near misses in exotic locations down the years: the Moroccan monster that got off the hook in Agadir, the Bulgarian nippers that nibbled but did not bite in the Black Sea, the *piranha blanca* that came off a chunk of meat in a dark and sultry tributary deep in the Peruvian jungles of Amazonia, the river where Fitzcarraldo hauled his boat all those years ago. What a story that fish would have told, had I caught him to tell it, of life in the waters of the *Madre de Dios* river. What names they have for rivers in South America.

6

East & South, Again

Ireland shrinks, so it seems. Ribbon-roaded with mo-torways, a legacy of the boom. Journey times have shortened and quickened, in all senses. From the tame Irish sea to the wild Atlantic Ocean is a mere two hours. Hardly a satisfactory stint float-fishing on a stream, but enough time to get from one side of the country to the other. The trouble with motorways is that it's difficult to spy good water from them, and harder still to persuade yourself to drive off smooth, sleek, straight surfaces and delay your arrival at wherever the destination is. Modern life is all about getting there. Fast.

Time was when the road from Dublin to Waterford or Cork was so slow and winding you could see the fish and their shadows in the rivers and canals down below, waving up, taunting and tempting you to stop and cast. The bridge over the Liffey in Kilcullen, for instance. Barry and I took three small brown trout, all on flies, downstream from the roadway arches after stopping for a while on the way home from Tramore. He landed a fine Grand Canal rudd on floating sweetcorn south of Monasterboice, off the Cork road, and three years later in the same canal south of Athy, a rudd each on maggots for both of us. In Kilkenny, a small brownie for Barry on a worm floated off the bridge at Thomastown.

At the same place almost a year later, on a stop-off on one of our interminable and innumerable trips to Tramore, he lifted a nice ten ounce rainbow trout, also on a worm. Three days later, on our way back to Dublin, we stopped in Thomastown again. This time we put our wellies on and walked in the water that swirled at the river's edge under the bridge. A wise move, resulting in a rainbow apiece for Barry and me, both three-quarter pounders on worms. A friendly local whispered as he walked on by, "The season isn't open yet, lads." Ooops. Also in Kilkenny, I took a quarter-pounder of a brownie on a Blue Dun at the weir below the bridge in Kells, where flows a famous tributary of the Nore called the King's River, which later wends its way through the grounds at Mount Juliet. Deeper south again, a tiddler brownie on a fly at the weir below the wooden bridge in Kilmacow. The river here is one of many in Ireland called the Blackwater. It is a tributary of the Suir, a certain sign that Munster, and the deepest south, is not far away.

So we were back in Waterford, a region not short on excellent trout rivers and streams. The county also holds lakes, reservoirs and, high in the Comeraghs, little gems of trout loughs that are on my radar though I have not fished them yet. I have seen them when hill-walking with Marie, shimmering in the valleys beneath the peaks of Coumfea and Comeragh Mountain. They wink and dazzle up at us, deep and dark and promising. From Ballyshunnock, a stocked reservoir out at Carroll's Cross Roads, came two fine fat brownies on floating worm, a two-pounder and a smaller one at one pound, nine ounces. Claire also successfully angled for stickleback here, delighting a passing bailiff who came to check our permit and stopped to chat for half an hour. Together we watched little flashes of stickleback underbelly as they turned and twisted in the water trying to cope with Claire's floating worm. Belle Lake, on the road to Dunmore East, is an easy spot to reel in a fish. Barry and Claire have taken rudd on maggots there. Cast a sprat lure in Belle Lake, spin it, and you are guaranteed to haul up a pike.

But nothing beats secluded, unspoilt riverbank. A bend in the flow with no sign of human habitation in front or behind, or on either side. No concrete, no construction, no artefact of man, to be seen anywhere. No *progress*, only endless time all around, enveloping you. Blue flash of kingfisher swoops over sparkling water, butterflies flitter across your gaze from nearby meadows. Branches green with leaves and pregnant with moss bend in supplication to passing currents. All this in your eyes. In your nostrils the sweet scent of honeysuckle, the strong smell of cow dung from a field behind you. In your ears the lowing of distant cattle, the sound of white water – sweet music, especially when standing on a riffle, cool feel of river swirling and clawing like a slithery cat round boots or waders, line cast into a glide, watching it flow downstream, pulling gently, guiding the fly or lure to a likely spot.

A flow in the shallows near a weed bed, or maybe a pool beneath overhanging trees. Wait for a tug. A quick strike and out comes a trout, perhaps a small one but size does not matter except to stat-obsessed match-fishers and trophy hunters. A speckled brown trout, mottled with evolution of millennia, red spots like rubies etched along the flanks. Hold the fish gently in your wet hand, remove the hook, admire your fish one last time, release him or her carefully in a shallow. Watch as the fish regains nerve, strength, bearings. See the fish dart away, gone. Cast again if you want. Then go, leave no trace so that no one will ever know you've been here, except the place itself – that secret location where you and nature engage, confer, and agree to part on mutually respectful terms.

Barry, Claire and I caught eleven golden trout, each like the fish described above, in the River Clodiagh near Portlaw, on two visits using floating worm and various flies. The last day of the season resulted in a small brownie plucked from the Tay just upstream of the bridge below the pretty village of Stradbally, on a Greenwell's Glory. Subsequent visits to the same place yielded a half dozen trout on Butchers and Black Pennells, including two at once when fishing a team of three wet flies downstream of the bridge. Barry landed a baby flounder to accompany my little brownie; both on worm ledgered in the River Mahon across the fields from Seafield school near Bunmahon. Plus a wildie on an orange-winged fly from the Dawn River below the restored railway bridge at Kilmeadan.

There exists a king among rivers, the Munster Blackwater, otherwise known as Ireland's Rhine. Maggot were the payload that floated beneath my stick-float – a technique known as trotting. The float bobbed up and down. I stood casting from the shore upstream of another railway bridge, this one at Cappoquin. A bailiff, not the man from Ballyshunnock, emerged from the bushes to check my permit. It was obvious from the tackle and set-up that game fish were not my target on this occasion. No dace permit required. We talked for a long time, bailiff and I, watching the float fall and rise, fall and rise. The local dace, delightful silvery fish, slim and sparkling, were biting. I caught four of them, this species which seems to be a speciality of the Blackwater. What better way to end a day like that than to stop in a roadside pub for a pint on the way home, if you can find a pub that has not closed its doors to business. The licensed trade has been devastated all over this part of county Waterford, likewise all areas of rural Ireland. The countryside is shutting down, thanks to the economic recession allied with the political correctness of the nanny state. One fishing trip that did end up in a pub visit turned out to be a visit earlier than intended.

It occurred one warm July day when Waterford hurlers were in the middle of yet another glorious, though ill-fated as always (so it seems), campaign to lift the All-Ireland title. The match was beamed live on television. Being a soccer fan at heart, the lure of the Annestown River proved a greater attraction than hurling. Annestown is a very unusual Irish village in that, in my twenty years of driving through the place, it appears to have no public house in its precincts. None at all. At least none that is visible. Annestown does possess a river, a magnet for mullet that flows down past the delightfully situated Dunhill Castle, a fairytale castle when seen from certain angles, in certain light. The Annestown River flows through an equally enchanting valley several miles inland to the east of Dunhill, which is another small village – this one does have a pub, a fine establishment, too.

The valley was a secret known only to the privileged few – now it is being waymarked and developed as an attraction for walkers. A few years ago access involved vaulting a farm gate at Ballyphilip Bridge, trudging past a cattle grid bridge that spans the Annestown, little more than a stream now, to where the second falls above the grid flows out from a deep, broad pool. Here I watched my float go under, no finer feeling, but struck too soon. The fish, heavy enough whatever it was, slipped off the hook – no greater feeling of frustration exists than that momentary loss. The sense of failure and loss soon passes and hope rises again, especially when the setting is as gorgeous as this. Higher upstream, where the valley opens out and takes your breath away with extended beauty, not to mention deer herds grazing on a hillside farm, I dangled a worm on the far side and thought I noticed the float glide a fraction *up*stream. A contra-flow is strange but could be caused by currents bobbing back off the bank. I looked again. The float was shifting *against* the grain of the river. I reeled in, feeling no weight at the end of the line. A phantom fish, probably. Then I saw the flashing of a tiny belly, and felt the slightest, most fleeting resistance in my hand.

I hauled him out, though *hauled* is hardly an appropriate verb, and saw that he had stuffed himself so full of worm he could not get free in time. It was a Waterford minnow. I released him, and smiled. Three hours with worms *and* fly rod had led to this, my catch of the day. Definitely time to pack the gear up and go. I checked my watch. If I put my skates on, the second half of the Waterford match would only just be starting by the time I got to the screen of Mother McHugh's pub in Fenor.

Exceptional warm April weather earlier that year led to the purchase of a new addition to the fishing arsenal – a kayak, a baby one, ideal for exploring the Copper Coast of County Waterford. This stretch of coastline is an area of cliff and seashore – a hidden Ireland – indented with caves, arches, sea stacks and rock formations almost entirely underexplored yet so exotic they have to be met up close to be fully appreciated, especially in a kayak so small it can venture into tight spaces that other, larger, craft cannot go near.

On a rare hot summer's day I lugged the kayak from the carpark at Saleen down to the weedy estuarine beach opposite Tramore dunes, launching seaward on the dying kick of an ebb-tide. Out into the channel, past the spot where Pepé and I landed that fine sea trout on a spinning bass lure, out past Rinnashark along the shore to Brownstown Head; the paddle dipped in silver sheen so still I could hear the gabble of mackerel men in a fishing boat though they drifted several hundred yards away. I let the kayak glide on a tide so low it floated beneath the low-water mark on a canopy of whole forests – oar-weed and bladder bloom; water so pure I reached down to caress fronds rarely, if ever, uncovered, and beheld the fronds adorned with pearls of roving periwinkles and sparkling arms of starfish.

I saw an opening and entered another world; nine feet four inch length of kayak echoed the cave's diameter with barely an inch to spare. Floating motionless, bereft of tide, watching light play dappled tricks on solid rock, I wondered had anyone ever been in here before? My long blade worked ancient stone, turning the kayak slowly, levering hull until bow faced starlit entrance. Outside, a canoeist sat in his thirteen-footer, glancing with envious eyes at my craft. Sometimes length is not everything. Hot sun beat down. I slid into an arch, a cathedral of rock. Slanting rays shone through gothic skylight, illuminating my glistening arms, neck and legs with more beads of heat. The gnomon shadow of a sea stack loomed. I made for welcome shade and found, in a hollow beneath an overhang, a tiny beach accessed only by seal pups and small waders; a beach slung so low it may have dried out for mere minutes at the ebb of every flow. The overhang formed a perfect hood, a crescent. I held my breath. This was a special place, an altar, a holy shrine witnessed only by the favoured few, a hammock in the rocks for mermaids.

Tide began to turn. I made the most by cutting a straight line beyond the sharp rocky islets to the west of Brownstown Head. From here I stared miles to starboard, mesmerised by juts of Copper Coast stretching spindly arms and rocky fingers here and there into shimmering sea-haze. Stunning, inaccessible shoreline places with wonderful, ancient, maritime names: Drumcappul, Illaunglass, Patsy Micil's Strand, Hawks Cliff, Isles of Icane, Barrel Strand, Carrickadurrish, Chair Cove, Poll a Roon; names that work a spell – names to die for. When I looked to port I saw ... Hook Head, the towers of Brownstown truly behind me. A growing swell beneath the hull filled my bones with the gnawing feeling that I was no longer in Tramore Bay but at sea. I saw lobster pots float yards away and remembered bobbing lobster markers of three brothers lost at this spot, their pots perhaps still dangling beneath floating tombstones. I heard the thunder of breakers crash into rocky buttresses and felt the urgent need to bow my head, partly in prayer, mainly to propel my paddle to seek the nearest, driest, comfort zone. I crabbed an unsteady and uncertain rum-line between the Head and those rocky islets I'd rounded on my way out, got the timing right and reached safety on the crest of a low-slung wave. Sheltered once again in the lee of the cradling arm of the bay, the tide now fully turned, the glide back to Saleen guaranteed and effortless. Yet more caves and inlets uncovered, undiscovered ...

But I digress, and must return to describing the kayak not for cruising, but as a fishing weapon.

I launched it once from Knockmahon Pier just west of the copper mines and paddled across Bunmahon Bay to Gull Island where mackerel surrendered to a jigged cod feather. For good measure I trolled yet another mackerel near the mouth of the River Mahon. The kayak has also served as a useful platform for a pollack jigged on feathers halfway between the pier at Tramore and the Guillamene. It folds in two and so fits into the hatchback of even a small car, making it possible to explore waters en route from Dublin or Waterford to wherever. The River Barrow, for instance.

A breezy summer's day; river surface free of wind because of shelter from banks either side. Ideal. There are days when rivers funnel breezes into upstream or downstream gales not conducive to good or safe kayaking, especially when paddling against the wind. This was no such day. Typical summer conditions: overcast with sunny intervals, not bad for a spin on the river. I parked the car in the grounds of Carlow Town Park and lugged the kayak to a slipway across from the new town riverfront happy in the knowledge that I had studied the Inland Waterways Association of Ireland's online maps of the Barrow Navigation. These maps are mines of information regarding location of slipways, landing stages, moorings, towpaths, weirs, navigation channels, bridges and correct archways to aim for when gliding under the bridges.

I knew it all, so I believed, paddling around islands of cygnets and ducklings, causing consternation and pandemonium among dragonflies so numerous it was like paddling through an Egyptian plague. Down to the town lock, then upriver past the rowing club. The refuge of nature beckoned. I paddled hard, churning water to escape this urban setting. On and on, past the ancient graveyard, under the road bridge, beneath the old sugar factory pipes that span the river. The sad old factory wharf, crumbling like our indigenous sugar industry. I passed an angler and paused briefly to cast out a small spinning lure. Trolling astern, I glided into a setting so sylvan and picturesque it was the stuff of kayak-dreams. My stroking eased now. I was where I wanted to be, a whole other world that can only be appreciated from the river when the surface is so smooth the glide no longer remains on water but goes on leaves and branches of upside-down trees reflected faithfully, reflected perfectly. It is hard to tell where tree ends and water begins. Landscape and waterscape meld into one huge oil painting, a living work of art. I let the kayak drift in figures of eight, losing myself to Mother Nature. It mattered not one jot that the fish were uncooperative. I paddled around a bend and saw where this section of the Barrow splits into river and canal.

The cutting for Bestfield Lock lay starboard of my bow a hundred yards in, lock gates closed against me. I paddled on regardless. The instinct to explore had taken over. Then I slowed. Something did not feel right. Something in the air around me; something I could feel and hear. Suddenly, lock gates loomed overhead. Millions of tons of water heaving against ancient timbers, yearning to break free, ready to crash down and kill. Then I identified what I was hearing – the sound of an engine chugging in the lock above. The air around me felt instantly, inappropriately, cold. A shiver sailed up the paddle arms into my heart. If there was a boater up there starting his engine, and I stayed put down here in a blind spot under the gates ...

I turned and paddled away, determined to escape a deluge, then strained my neck to look over my shoulder. Had I really heard the sound of a boat's engine up there? Could it have been a weird, hallucinatory effect caused by the rustle of the breeze through trees combined with noise of water sluicing through gaps in the rotting timbers of the lock gates? Could it have been a crazy fear similar to the irrational urge to leap off the platform's edge when a train approaches? Slowing now, knowing I had safe distance on my side, I paddled back into the river and glided upstream to a point level with the lock gates. I beached the kayak, stepped ashore on the riverbank and peered across at the canal. I could see no boat from my view through the trees. Looking downstream, no vessel emerged from the cutting. There had been no engine. I shrugged, re-launched and paddled back down to Carlow, forgetting about the lock and mysterious engine sound. The charm of the Barrow, the elegance of that graceful flow, held me in its thrall. As for traffic, only one craft, a motorboat, passed in the two hours I was afloat. Back at the slip, I folded up the kayak and resumed my car journey to Dublin.

That night I re-opened the IWAI Barrow Navigation maps on my home computer, to retrace the day's kayaking. This time I was not bothered with location of slipways, landing stages, moorings, towpaths, weirs, navigation channels, bridges and correct archways. I knew where these were now. I had seen them with my eyes that day. Now my concentration shifted from the visuals to the written information, which I had neglected to read on my earlier visit. My eyes flitted from the diagrams on the left side of the screen to the text on the right-hand side of Barrow Navigation Map 7 – Carlow – and saw nothing unusual in the text columns there. Factual, historical information. Then I clicked on Map

6 – Bestfield Lock. The following words jumped out of the screen at me:

> *Bestfield Lock is reputed to be haunted. In the days of commercial traffic the boatmen spoke of strange happenings such as knocking on the hulls of the canal boats at night.*

I could not believe what I was reading. The manifestation I had witnessed that day, if it had been a vestige of something supernatural, had been aural in nature, like the auditory example I had just read about in the text column on the IWAI map. I've since tried to investigate Bestfield both online and in book form, but have unearthed little information beyond the basic fact that the canal is reputed to be haunted by a nineteenth century haulier who drowned at the lock.

Whether or not there existed that July day any firm basis, any real *connection* between the hollows of my mind and something not of this world, I do not know. What occurred that summer afternoon on the Barrow was probably just a trick of sound played out in my foolish head. A wall of water loomed over me, causing my imagination to run away with itself; that same old writerly imagination that can take something simple – a kayak, for example – and turn it into the worst thing that could possibly be imagined, which is exactly what happens in the dark story that follows, "Water, Some of It Deep". I hasten to add that this next chapter is totally the product of a fevered literary imagination. Any resemblance between characters within its dread-filled pages and persons living or dead is completely coincidental and non-intentional.

7

Water, Some of It Deep

Memories of Henry swirl in my head like sawdust at a woodcutter's. In his fifties, he seemed a man with everyday interests: backing horses, model aircraft, writing poetry. Not to mention canoeing. Or was it kayaking? – I don't know the difference. He could be wonderfully entertaining. Words tumbled from the magnificent shambles of his mind, his mouth never slow with an opinion. He brimmed with conversation and a bubbly wit too complex for most of the West Cork locals. They disliked his shuffling demeanour, the intensity behind those round-rimmed spectacles, the brooding hints that beneath that chaotic grey hair lurked depths they could not fathom. Around here they prefer their ageing hippies to be simple, readable, predictable – something to lend a little colour to the landscape. Henry was none of those things.

I first met him six years ago after Fiona and I moved west out of the city to live by the coast. We had always

wanted to live by the sea – she to paint, I to write poetry. Or as the real world would have it: she part-timed
as a school secretary, I worked nixers in interior design.
Our community here was small, a few hundred souls in
a scattering of houses nestled along a cove. Three pubs,
a couple of shops – a street of sorts that looked well in
summer, though not many tourists veered off the main
drag to come here. We were off road and, more often
than not, off season. On dark days, especially in bad
light of winter, our houses and street, no matter how
brightly painted, took on a drab, nondescript look.

Henry's wife, Ursula, had become friendly with
Fiona despite a generation gap. My wife was twenty-
nine, Ursula fifty-one. Henry had nineteen years on
my thirty-eight. We shared four-sided dinners in their
cottage, sometimes in ours. He loved a good intellec-
tual exchange. So did I. We sought each other out, for
a while. People left us to ourselves. In my early days
here, one of our few mutual friends let slip that his pals
had asked him, when he had returned to their company after half an hour drinking with Henry and me,
why he bothered "talking to those fellas". So we were
known as "those fellas" with the emphasis on "those"
as if we were a newly discovered social disease. Henry
did not care what people thought. Neither, at first, did
I. Sometimes people asked me on the street or when I
was holding up a bar, "How can you stand yer man?"

I shrugged my shoulders, made vague replies. "He's
not too bad. He's not the worst."

One night in bed a few years ago, after dinner at Henry's, Fiona lay in the crook of my arm. "Henry's fixated by the financial crisis, isn't he?" she said. "Did he lose much in the crash?"

"I dunno, love. He hates bankers."

"He has lots of pet hatreds."

Pet hatreds? They were becoming more like Rottweilers. Fiona's comment struck me as rich considering how friendly she was with the sharp-tongued Ursula. "He hates bankers," I said, "becauses he's a child of the sixties who can't stand greed and materialism. He's just a cranky old hippy."

"Cranky is right. Listening to him giving out about the world tonight was worse than spending an hour watching a current affairs programme on economics."

"And it lasted just as long," I said, putting my hand on her shoulder, pulling her close.

Now I sigh and stretch in my empty bed. Dust of memory comes at me in a blizzard. I wear no goggles to keep stinging, eye-gouging memories at bay. I wear, as I have worn for years, a pair of blinkers. I should have seen that he needed to be in control, not mundanely as a control freak, which he was, but because his mind was growing erratic to the point of *demanding* control over everything, not just his own life, of the world around him. No aura of creepiness clung to him, though I see now that I was complicit in the evil that lurked beneath his chummy veneer. His intensity, his combativeness, his need to confront, led to him becoming unable to pull back. I should have read the signs and seen it coming because over the last few years of our friendship he had begun to paw the ground intellectually, looking for arguments, seeking out spats, putting his head down in such bullish fashion that it culminated in four arguments in two hours.

On the night of those arguments, twelve months ago now, I had known him less than five years. Several times in our history I had considered dropping his friendship, our relationship having gone through more than one cooling-off period. Each time I allowed him back in because I would warm to him again by convincing myself that life would be poorer without him, which it would have been in the same way as war would be poorer without all those deaths.

The first disagreement must have been a trivial matter – I cannot recollect it. The second argument began when I said I liked the latest piece of popular music sweeping the land. He called me a "musical ignoramus". I thought that a little strong and argued the toss before veering the conversation to another topic. He made equally strong comments on the state of the country. I considered what he was saying to be dangerous generalisations. While I can take criticism of my country, there are still a few nationalist hackles – genetically installed at conception, I believe – that rise when the dressing-down comes from the lips of an Englishman. I looked around the bar wishing for someone else, anyone, to join us. It was the fourth and final row that clinched it. At closing time I began telling him of poetry readings lined up to coincide with my book launch. He said, "It just goes to show that you don't need a high standard of work to get a collection published these days."

I felt that my innards had been filleted. It may only have been a small, independent publisher in the city but it was legitimate and Arts Council funded and paying me a pittance unlike the two vanity presses *he* had paid to bring out his collections in England. I would get reviews and invites to arts festivals and be regarded as a genuine player on the circuit. He never would. He knew that and it killed him, and he knew that I knew how he secretly felt, but it still killed *me* to hear him say those ugly words. I sat there like an imploded corpse, wondering where the Henry I had met five years ago had gone, the man of wit and charm replaced now by an intellect cold, judgemental, willing to say something that he should never have said, to jettison the friendship of half a decade for what – an opinion? In one of those fate-ordained moments Old Colm stood behind the counter with his hands on his hips. "One for the ditch, lads?"

"Why not? Two pints of your finest stout!"

"I'm okay," I said. "I've had enough."

Henry grasped the seriousness of his final insult only when I refused an after-hours drink.

He and Old Colm stared at me, both stunned into silence. Over the next minutes Henry tried to shallow-gossip about everyday things. I finished my drink and lifted my jacket off the back of the stool. He downed his pint and accompanied me to the door as if nothing had happened. Stepping outside, I looked at him and said, "See you around, Henry."

We parted and went our separate ways. My belly sloshed with the slop of sour stout. My mind tipped over with the firm intentions of never allowing myself to sit in that man's company again.

Next day he went out in his canoe as he did most days. I often visualise him in that pathetic little vessel. I prefer that to picturing him in other activities those final, awful weeks. I see him now on his last day. I re-play that day over and over, not wanting events of oth-er days to come into my mind. I give him thoughts to complement his actions – harmless thoughts, zany ac-tions – merely harmless, merely zany. Early symptoms of an insane mind. His or mine? Sometimes I wake up in a sweat and think: I am no longer sure.

I see him launch his canoe. He jumps aboard glimpsing from the corner of his eye a page of his log-book hanging loose on the prow. He recalls yesterday's entry, remembering it word-perfect:

From Bramble Head to Bluff Harbour. About three and a half miles. Light sou'westerly. Otherwise flat calm. Must remember to stow sun-cream on board

in future. Fished for codling on the drift,
no luck. Went ashore at Dudgeon Cove.
No annoying jet-skis today.

He pulls hard on the paddle before the swell pushes him back onto sand. A few strokes take him beyond suck of beach. With his paddle across his midriff, he strains forward to tuck his precious logbook beneath its plastic cover to protect it from what salts and sprays the sea might throw. He has not revealed the log's existence to anyone, not even to Ursula and certainly not to me. Ironic that I, months later, should gain access to all his writings, nautical, poetic and otherwise. I make him look forward to thinking how tonight's entry might look. I imagine it for him:

Along the curve of Two-Mile Strand to
Ratchett Head. Across the bay on a ris-
ing tide.

Already the sun has burned holes in lace-curtain mist hanging over a flat Atlantic.

Ideal conditions for ocean-going.

He turns, pursues a course parallel to the shore. I make him sail slowly. I want to prolong it. With his long grey hair he glides through the mist, a pony-tailed Neptune caressing the surface with a double-ended blade.

The red cab of a tractor flashes at him from behind trees on the shore road. A silhouette in the bouncing cab salutes him, whether in jest or mockery Henry is not sure. I make him unsure because I want him to feel nervy, uncertain. He waves back though he suspects that the salute must be one of mockery. Because of his canoeing, locals had taken to saying, "Here's Henry the Navigator!" whenever he entered Old Colm's, a habit he had got out of in the year since our arguments. Deep down Henry had only contempt for the locals. I also have nothing but contempt for those around me, then and now.

"Navigator" was merited. "You're canoeing more as a career than a hobby," Ursula had said to him, her acid eloquence reminding him of why, in far-off college days, her fellow-students had given her a nickname of her own: "The Knife". This I know because he told me back in our friendlier days. What Ursula said was right: he had a compulsion for water, for the sea. If the weather was poor he paddled on wind-sheltered lakes and rivers.

He imagines a sea-area forecast in a plummy, old-fashioned BBC accent.

> *Fastnet: cloud increasing. Pressure fall-*
> *ing. Wind strong to gale force. Visibility*
> *zero. Small craft warning in operation.*
> *All ferry services cancelled.*

Hugging the shoreline that last, fateful morning, his mood sours to match his imagined shipping news. I make a dread feeling stalk him in a vital, hidden spot.

He must have experienced it many times, this dangerous imitation of dangerous weather.

*Henry: Happiness falling. Storm clouds
gathering. Outlook gloomy. Prospects
zero. All future services cancelled.*

A sudden lurch almost topples him over. Concentrate, he tells himself, looking around for the rogue
wave that had caught him unawares. He sees a swell
so gentle he has to look for it. He suspects there might
be something beneath his hull. Guilt? He looks over
the side. Nothing but shelving sand scarcely a fathom
deep. He begins to feel his blood warm up and thinks of
what might have been – and had been, twice – tucked
in the storage space behind him. There is nothing there
now, nothing to slip sideways and unbalance his canoe.
I make the sun come out. It warms his back by the time
he turns seaward at Ratchett Head.

Across the bay on a rising tide ...

to his last port of call. That special spot, a hiding place
on the southern side of an east-facing cove. Henry feels
better where beach surrenders to a rocky coastline of
caves, coves, stacks and sea arches. So much more in-
teresting than endless sand: these overhanging cliffs to
paddle under. Little chance of eyes prying from above,
many hiding places secret and inaccessible.

He looks around. No lobstermen out in boats this
ripple-free morning, no nosey trawlers or kayaking

tourists. Good. He canoes close to bearded rocks, no longer part of the servile world beyond the cliffs, the land of greed, selfishness and materialism; the world that had robbed him of his wealth in the recession, and turned its critical back on his poetry. One lot had cheated him of his money. The others would not know good poetry if it rose up and bit them in the arse. This he thinks. This I know. He said it to me. Fuelled by resentment and paranoia, ignited by a double blow – one financial, the other artistic – his head had tipped over into rage, vengeance and an all-consuming need to strike out at what society held to be its most precious cargo – its future. I can only think that his toxic slow burn had smouldered for months, years, before bursting into fire those last crazy weeks. On this sunny final day he no longer feels as if his brain and heart might explode with fury and violence at any moment. Now he feels light-headed because he is sailing away from the world of greed and fear. Looking up at the sky beyond the cliffs he believes that the world beneath that cruel blue lid is no longer real. *This* is what is real, he tells himself: the bright seaward side of the cliffs – ocean, sun and sparkle.

He sees spray of sprat on a sunlit surface, mackerel chasing them from below. He witnesses visions of garfish in pursuit, of wrasse wrestling with weeds and crustaceans. He is glad to have left his rod at home. No morning for fishing, this. No day for interfering with the natural order. I imagine another entry for his log, one that turns out to be true.

> *A day of consequence, of restoration and reparation, a time of atonement after weeks of insanity. Funny how the mind behaves under pressure. Now the pressure recedes.*

He paddles on, leaving fish to consume themselves. He thinks: this is how it is up and down the food chain all the way from gannets squealing overhead to molluscs slugging it out on the ocean floor. And larger predators too – sharks and killer whales, not to forget those gliding along the surface in hulls long and sleek, the width of a coffin, the same colour as a coffin, pointed at both ends for stealth and sleekness. He hugs the coastline. He glides around a series of rocks to slide under a vulva-like arch, a portal to another world. Scrag Rock hoves into view, beyond it Tern Island. He is close now, within a gull's midnight scream. On his port side, sunlight illumines the sea with a glare to hurt his eyes. He blinks, keeps his gaze forward, slides past familiar boulders and kelpbeds drowned in rising tide. He looks around, spellbound. The sea is a heaven-sent mirror reflecting the beauty of nature. That last morning was one made for canoeing, a morning sent from God. Henry had often gone looking for God. He was looking for God a long time. He wanted to talk to Him.

To his starboard, rocks open up, revealing a small creek in the cliff, a tiny stream-hewn cove inaccessible from above.

> *Two strokes of the paddle take me across an ocean of pain. I should have been a terrorist, a mere terrorist. I would have preferred that, and willingly taken it, had You seen fit to give me a choice.*

A small crevice, big enough to line himself up with the confidence that a canoeing man will fit. An expert swish of the blade, a stoop of the head; he is in. He stops the canoe and turns smoothly through three-sixty degrees. Reflected sunlight from the entrance creates an eerie dappled effect on a small dome-shaped cave just large enough for his twelve-foot craft. He looks down on dark blue water full of anemones, invertebrates, blennies, shrimps and other harmless creatures. He checks the state of the tide. He has ten minutes before it begins to rise and he will have to leave. He looks up. The dancing light from the entrance stipples the rock above the waterline with the ghostly marbled echo of light and all things bright. This is a wall haunted by algae, limpets, winkles, crabs and other scavengers. They climb with advancing tides, and sometimes of their own greedy, slithery crawl, to a ledge above the high-water mark, a ledge you would never think was there unless you knew where to look, a place large enough to hide something from the eyes of all the world.

Henry's narrow, brown eyes adjust to the dim stipple of cave-light. He lifts the paddle over his head and places it behind his back at right angles across the canoe. He feels his breath come shallow and fast, not from exertion but because he is about to see his handiwork. Pressing down on the paddle with his wrists he straightens his arms, lifts his buttocks off the canoe-seat and raises his head to ledge level. He opens his mouth to drink in the damp air. His eyes widen. He has to have one last look.

I no longer want to think about that day.

If I said I had not spoken to him since the Night of the Four Arguments, it would not be true. Our paths did cross. Whatever words we exchanged were polite greetings, nothing more. He took to staying in his cottage, so it seemed. I realised then that it was mutual, the desire to end our friendship. I was glad of that. So was Fiona. She had always found him hard to stomach. She remained friendly with Ursula, though we dined no more at Henry's. Our wives met for coffee or went shopping in the city. I rarely found myself in Ursula's company. The same could be said of Fiona and me. We passed each other by in the narrowing confines of our lives. Though the cottage was small, its rooms may have been wide-open spaces for all the companionship there was between us.

For some time I had felt her growing resentment that she was carrying me, her salary paying for my poetry. Her family felt the same: frittering away her life and money on a semi-bohemian waster of a husband. Whatever Fiona and I had in common had eroded to little or nothing. She no longer painted. Watercolours had been for her a hobby but for me poetry was a compulsion. I had to write. She worked full-time as local school secretary now, the idealism of our earlier hopes buried among the dried-out easels in her paint-box. She no longer slept in the same bed as me, never mind in my arms. In those last twelve months my marriage plumbed like a depth charge longing to go off. During that year-long period I believed that Henry had no influence on the state of my worsening relationship with Fiona. Like so many other things those sad, dreary days, I was wrong about that too.

When the first child disappeared, the school where Fiona worked became a hornet's nest of sideways glances, accusatory looks, tension so concrete you could riverdance on it. She took the worst of it, more than the teachers or the principal. Fiona was in the foremost trench – the secretary's office being first in the firing line between school and a demented world of parent-crazy, media-driven frenzies of fear, charge and counter-charge. We thought it would die down as the weeks crawled by. It got worse. News vans everywhere, you could not walk down the street without someone sticking a microphone under your nose. Fiona was like a bag of ferrets each day after work. I saw it get to her.

It got to me. I saw us all undermined as weeks slid by and the child's body was never found. Henry was high on the list of suspects mentioned in despatches in the pub. The local know-alls had monitored how he had cut back his visits to Old Colm's.

"Henry the Navigator's gone very odd," one of them said to me one night at the bar counter.

"In what way?"

"He doesn't come out much any more. He's gone too quiet."

"Maybe that's because the last time he was in, you and your buddies called him Henry the Navigator to his face and laughed him out of it."

That killed the conversation. I finished my pint thinking that Henry's habit of shooting from the hip had rubbed off on me, which made me none too popular that night. I was glad because there was too much rumour-milling going on, yet I could not help but think these rumours were true. Henry had gone strange – going out canoeing in all weathers. When I mentioned this to Fiona, who throughout the child tragedy remained friendly with Ursula, she glared at me.

"God knows we've enough to worry about. Is that all you can think about? *Him?*"

All my exchanges with Fiona had become like that: short duels with verbal bullets. We were taking pot shots at each other at the end of every sentence. There was no warmth, only brief meetings over what was, or more frequently was not, in the fridge or kitchen cupboard, or the use of the car and other unavoidable swapping of practical information. Then off we went ducking and diving down sniper's alley, our rubble of a marriage demolished by years of bad communication and bad love.

Five weeks after the first, the second child was taken. Also nine years old, also a girl. The sky had fallen with the first disappearance. With the second, the gravitational impact of all the planets made my neighbours' shoulders sag, caused their eyes to ooze with suspicion and mistrust. Everyone who was still sane seemed crushed with worry and guilt. Each time I looked they stared back, faces fuelled with the fear of what might happen next – and who might be doing it. Detectives and uniforms searched everywhere, as did the locals. Teams of volunteers, including Henry, walked bogs, mountains and coastline. Everywhere and everything was searched, but the trainee-policeman who looked inside Henry's canoe to make sure that it was empty failed to check it with a DNA kit. A single hair, fluid or skin sample would have solved it all. Days and weeks dragged on. Fiona aged a decade those two witless months. With no bodies and no arrests, a scapegoat had to be found. The communal and police-procedural finger pointed at a simple-minded twenty-three year old from a nearby village, an unfortunate victim of an accident on the first day of his one and only job as a butcher's apprentice. He had hacked all four fingers off his left hand in the butcher's shop when he was fourteen years old. "Stumpy" the locals had christened him. That he walked around with porn DVDs sticking out of his back pocket made him public enemy number one. He was arrested and dragged off, chased by a howling mob.

That last day returns to haunt me. I see him crouch. His bowed head misses the overhanging rock by inches. He is out. A swish of blade propels him from his private altar, abandoned now to its dome-shaped cathedral of stone, protected for all time by secrecy of sea, tide and cliff. He paddles across an ocean of pain. The sea has him surrounded. His mind overflows with the mother of all log entries, his canoe slowed by the weight of stones he has picked up in that creek in the cliff.

Stardate 5432 point 1 ...

he sniggers and considers how the human mind is capable of dwelling on gross flippancy and immeasurable regret at the same time. He wishes he could sit on a barstool and debate such matters with ... it doesn't matter now. He must have felt remorse. His mind surely was tortured, given what happened next. I grasp at the hope that he did feel some shame, some twinge. He *must* have, given the log entries etched in my mind.

Mist returns. It covers him in its shroud.

Across the bay on a rising tide.

Is he paddling across the bay? He hopes not. He wants *out* of the bay. After all, he wrote:

Ideal conditions for ocean-going.

It is a good calm day for sailing into the broad Atlantic. Draped in mist, no one notices a single canoeist make his way out into the deep. He considers the mist to be as intangible as all the intangibles of his life, yet it is as enveloping, as consuming, as the most clear-cut, most formative events he can remember. He recalls all those definitive events now, as if enumerating them for his log, as if allowing them to wrap him up in one last personal shipping forecast. I imagine him writing:

Visibility zero. Pressure falling. Cloud dissipating. Outlook one of immense relief. Prospects much better for the world at large, and for the school-going population in particular.

He permits himself one last smile. His throat dries at what lies ahead. He determines to hold his course at all costs.

To thine own resolve be true ...

he writes, knowing that soon, very soon, he will talk to God. He feels the swell beneath his hull and welcomes it. He knows the wind will rise – from a zephyr to a gale. He wonders what height of wave his canoe can take. He told me once, that on the manufacturer's scale of one to ten, it could take only six. With long grey hair slung back Henry glides through the mist, once again a pony-tailed Neptune caressing the surface with double-ended sculls.

There were no more child disappearances. A sense of calm returned to the community, to Fiona, even to my marriage. In each case it was surface gloss, false as plastic fishing lures. Cracks have a habit of staying; I should know. I tried not to walk on them with Fiona. I would have needed to be a contortionist.

One day two months after her husband had disappeared, Ursula called to our door. She had about her a perfunctory look. There was a brusqueness in her manner that Fiona put down to the strain of her husband's suicide. We knew he had taken his own life because two days after Eoin O'Sullivan, the last person to see him alive, had waved to him from the cab of his tractor, Henry's body had been dragged up in a trawler's net. The man had made a crude attempt to weigh himself down by wrapping his paddle leash, weighed down by stones, around his upper body. Had the net not found him he might never have floated. His wife confirmed what Fiona and I already knew: they had lost all their savings in the market crash. The mortgage on their cottage was insurmountable, but there were other concerns. Ursula admitted that she was finding the going hard around here. One or two tongues wagged to the tune of how the child disappearances had stopped with her husband's death. Maybe the detectives had got the wrong man.

"Here," she handed me a folder full of spiral-bound poetry notebooks and other jotters. "You may as well have these. Nobody else would want his poetry anyway."

I was tempted to tell her how appropriate her college-day nickname had been. What I did was look at a knife on the kitchen table.

In days that followed, I examined Henry's poetry. Though the rhythm was correct and language adequate, his technique was cold, flat and clumsy. The lights were on in his head but the windows to his soul remained curtained. I decided to read everything including his canoeing logs. Ursula had handed me over the log he had written on his last day while drifting out on the tide. Crumpled and sea-stained, it was recovered from his pocket and remained legible, just, because of its tight plastic cover.

Some of the early logs were entertaining and revealing, especially his description of a freak wave capsizing him in Capalborus Bay. That day he had lost binoculars, compass, jacket, hat, pullover, sunglasses, mobile phone, boat rod, tackle box, lunchbox, hipflask, paddle, and very nearly his life, yet he still persevered with watery pursuits. My admiration for his determination soon soured. Later logs, especially the last one, bordered on the juvenile, a strange concoction of the real and unreal world inside his head, an amalgam of poetry, religion and, of all things, shipping forecasts. When I read a series of what I can only describe as poem-logs that he had called "Cargo", it was as if a foghorn went off in my brain. I could feel his paper shake in my cold fingertips as I read what he had written.

There were hints, geographical inferences. A number of the poem-logs centred on a place on the southern side of an east-facing cove near a small creek "two paddle-strokes" wide. Whatever distance paddle-strokes might be, his description narrowed things down. All the caves had been searched, how thoroughly I did not know.

I sat at a table in Old Colm's the next day. I knew Shamie would be in to drink his dole money. I spread an ordnance survey map in front of me and pretended to study it. Shamie was one of those locals who loved to show blow-ins that they would never know the landscape and seascape as well as he did. The map drew him like a mackerel to a sprat.

"I have a few friends coming down," I lied. "They love hillwalking, but I was thinking cliff walks might be just the thing for them."

"A change is as good as a rest," he said with a slow belch.

"I'd like to show them something spectacular along the cliffs. Tell me, Shamie, you'd know this. Are there any blowholes in the rocks around here?"

He looked at me from under bushy eyebrows. "There was the one at Capalborus Point. You could hear it ten miles away donkey's years ago, but it's been eroded by the waves. Still works but only on very rough days."

"I'll show them the caves and arches instead. They're not marked on the map. Where are the best ones?"

He pulled the map around to examine it closely.

I could contain myself no longer. "I know where some of the bigger caves are, looking down from my own walks. Are there any smaller ones that might be hidden by the tide?"

"They were all searched."

He had me rumbled but I persevered. "What about little ones that you'd never know were there? I bet there's very few around here." I pointed in the vague direction of Ratchett Head. A likely east-facing cove with an appropriate creek.

"Poulanconkary." He rose to it like a salmon, even putting his finger on the spot.

My Irish was rusty. *Poll an Choncaire* – the conger's lair? The name diced my insides.

"It was searched," he repeated. "Now, my city-boy friend, do you know something the rest of us don't?"

"Who searched it?"

"The local sub-aqua club."

"Did the Garda sub-aqua or naval divers search it?"

"They worked other places up and down the coast."

"So it was searched by a *club*?"

"Yes." Shamie's brow was as furrowed as Eoin O'Sullivan's field.

"Sunday divers," I said.

The man did not get it. He stared right through me.

I wangled my way out after buying him and his cronies a few whiskies. I never darkened Old Colm's door again. Weeks, months, after Stumpy's arrest, there was always one of them to say, "Who fingered Stumpy?" At that they would cackle like backyard hens.

I approached a local detective and told him my theory. He contacted the sub-aqua unit. They found the ledge and the remains of the two missing girls.

My life became unbearable once local papers got wind of it. When Fiona realised that her husband had been a paedophile's best friend she was back with her mother in Cork. Whether Henry was a paedophile or a child murderer I do not know. The bodies were more than two months dead and too damaged by decay and the crabs for the pathologist to tell. Distinctions between child murderer and paedophile are not observed or recognised around here. A rock through my front window was all the incentive I needed to move out. Stumpy had to leave also. He moved to England when they let him out of prison.

Ursula blamed Henry's financial troubles for wrecking the insides of his head. Strikes me as simplistic. When the real identity of the culprit broke, the poor woman could only clutch at straws. Last I heard she was walking the streets of Cork with a piece of string around her waist to keep her coat closed. Ursula has all the makings of becoming a bag lady. In my case Henry contributed to the break-up of my marriage. Not by the traditional act of sleeping with another man's wife – he did worse than that – but his actions were the catalyst for the break-up because, had I not been friendly with him, perhaps Fiona and I could have patched things up. I also clutch at straws.

His most secret character remains a mystery; his dark side an enigma. In dead of night I wonder can a personal monetary disaster tip an otherwise sane man from being normal – and normality is so relative – into the abyss? Was it like the last drop falling into a deep and hidden beaker of turmoil that finally turned him to the more horrific end of the human spectrum – that and facing up to the truth that his poetry would never make the grade? I don't know. I'm no expert. Experts are not much help. Police, psychiatrists, the press; nobody has a clue what stoked and fired him. He had never exhibited an unhealthy interest in the vulnerable or the young. He was not on the sex-offenders list in England. He had no previous of any sort. I must stop making excuses for this monster of a man.

I suffer recurring nightmares. All the manikin-children from all the clothes shops become animated. They zombie-march through the streets to my front gate, up the path, into my porch, up my stairs ... I wake up sweating, screaming, re-living that last day through Henry's narrow, beady eyes. Could I have saved those girls?

I miss Fiona. I fight against the bottle. I fight against myself. I have not been asked to do a reading since the murder story broke. I no longer write poetry. I keep a diary in the form of a log of a life destroyed by the accidental alignment of two lives, his and mine. In my attempts to understand the man and his motives I wonder what it is that draws people together. Are friendships accidental alignments? For instance, Henry's and mine? Do such friendships form in an instant glance? A certain set to the mouth? An openness of the palm? A glint in the eye? A willingness to listen? A mutual interest? That last bit worries me. I have no interest in avenging myself on the vulnerable or on the young but I feel cheated by circumstances that make me also want to gain revenge by wreaking havoc on all those happy people who surround me but stay well outside my walls. I am a loose cannon. There is madness in us all. It lies there, deep down, waiting its moment, itching to be switched on.

I live in the midlands now. I avoid tabloid journalists. I no longer read newspapers. I sit in a dirty, one-roomed flat flexing my wrists, unable to remove from my mind the tragedy of those girls. I stare into the mirror at eyes narrow and brown, just like Henry's. I feel his pain.

There are lakes around here. I walk their shorelines. I am beginning to like these inland expanses of water. I am drawn to the sheen of the lakes, as Henry was drawn to the sparkle of the sea.

8

South & West

What better way to raise the mood, to release the bubbles of the spirit and float the heavy heart from a deep abyss of trouble and inhumanity, than to head south. Raise a glass in salute to poetry and a hymn to fishing called "Tackle":

> *With dreams of monsters lurking deep*
> *we cast our hooks out from the shore*
> *and settled down to drink our beer.*
>
> *The day grew still, our lines fell slack,*
> *two floats inert, the light so bright*
> *off came our shirts: we soaked the sun*
>
> *and lay there like a pair of seals*
> *working on tans of winter pale,*
> *observing how the vapour trail*

that crossed the sky was not a patch
on the dragonfly that glistened
blue iridescence, leaf to leaf.

We smoked a toke and raised our cans
to the women in our lives and cursed
the government for all the lies.

We changed our bait to no avail.
When hunger struck you handed me
a roll of beef and chocs so sweet

no restaurant could ever match
the ambience of lakeside feast.
Hours came and hours passed in

tales of books and new releases.
We caught no fish – what did it matter?
We fixed the problems of the world

and thought that all was well until
you revealed your secret worry
which I pretended not to know

though everyone already knew.
In setting sun we packed our rods
and we fixed that, too.

Going deeper south is easy from Tramore – we are almost there already. Point the car west eighty miles on a good road, the N25. An hour and a half from Waterford to Cork brings us back at the Lough. To begin, though, the small matter of fishing locations along the way, and a celebration of the sea.

On feathers from the promenade at Green Park in Youghal: two pollack, a solitary mackerel, another pollack for Barry. Off the pier at Ballycotton, one mackerel and a green-tinged, silver-scaled sprat that tasted of the succulence of the sea once we filleted him in classic style by slicing around the gills and pulling the head away. Bones, attached to the head, came out cleanly. The fish was ready, frying pan waiting.

From the rocks at Church Bay a greedy pollack ambushed one of our feathers. He erupted out of a stormy wave like a sea-to-air missile, flanks of bronze shimmering in the sun as he flew skywards. We admired his curved lateral line, the protruding lower jaw gasping, gills open as we prepared to throw him back to the kingdom whence he came. In a gulley in limpet-covered rocks at our feet, detritus of tide and storm had washed up thousands of yellow and white periwinkles that lay heaped on each other, their shape and colour reminding me of miniature yellow and white construction helmets also discarded now – detritus of a construction industry laid low by corrupt politicians, inept bankers, greedy speculators and developers. Strange the thoughts that fill the head, stranger still in a stunning place like this. Soon the sun broke through again, heralding better thoughts and memories. Across from the stony shore at Church Bay lie the rocks of Roche's Point. Just down from the lighthouse, another pollack, possibly a cousin of the one just released, took a spinning German Sprat lure.

Roche's Point is a proper headland that juts its nose into the Atlantic. No click of urban heel on rocks hereabouts, no scuff of sand on mile after mile of strand – there is no mile-long beach. These are not lapdog waters that come in on gentle swells to lick a tame shoreline, as is often the case with the Irish Sea – a poodle-sea that, more often than not, laps mere ripples on the east coast. Here the waves bare their teeth in a frothing snarl, three-thousand mile rollers often rabid with rage cleave the rocks, cleanse the land and subdue the coastline with their silver blood. These are the wild wolf waves of the west.

One July day, Barry and I bumped into Denis in the hotel at Crosshaven during oyster festival time. He said to us, "Would you like to come out in my boat?"

A second invitation was not required.

Next day, August 1, we motored out from the Salve Marine marina in Crosser; our vessel a thirty-six foot converted fishing trawler, our goal the Sovereign Rocks in search of ling and conger. The Sovereigns lie some forty feet down, wreck-strewn, a haunt for all sorts of prey. The fish proved uncooperative, though Denis did reel in a small conger. A fine boat rod rigged up with a

Penn Senator reel, worth about two hundred pounds at the time, went flying over the side. Denis had left it to rest against the boat rail instead of securing it in a rod holder. Whether the hook had been taken by something big, or merely snagged on rocks, we will never know. Trolling for its return proved fruitless. We steered for the harbour. Off Fountainstown, and in the channel between the forts, the mackerel were throwing themselves aboard. We hauled in over a hundred. Barry took sixty-five, I pulled thirty-nine; some consolation for Denis and the loss of his rod. That evening we consoled ourselves further in the Admiral Drake. When sympathetic locals heard about the loss of the rod and Penn reel, they looked at each other between ever-narrowing eyelids. Trolling would have been a popular activity around the Sovereigns next morning.

The site of the Sovereigns may be viewed, from a distance, over at the Old Head of Kinsale, scene of more rod woe though not as serious as what befell Denis and his expensive equipment. On a fine summer's day, Marie, Barry and Claire relaxed on the nearby beach at Garretstown while I wandered off, mackerel hunting. Together with a few lads on a day out from the city, we slithered and slipped our way down to a location inaccessible now that the Head has been turned into an exclusive golf club that caters for those privileged enough to afford an expensive green fee.

We found ourselves on a rocky outcrop, a fine platform for casting. Only then did I discover that the bale arm on my reel had broken on the hectic scramble down to the shore. All I could do was sit and watch my companions reel in mackerel after mackerel – no spare reel in my tackle bag or in theirs. After a short time I clambered disconsolately back to where I had parked the car, extracted a small telescope from a compartment in the dashboard, leaned on the bonnet and focussed on the rocks below. They were still reeling them in, mackerel after bloody mackerel. I returned to the sand at Garretstown. Marie had the gas stove ready, but Man-the-Hunter returned fishless.

Game fishing has produced the odd result off the N25 on various Cork-Waterford journeys. In the Dungourney River just below the Old Youghal Bridge in Midleton, intense aroma of whiskey from the nearby distillery heavy in my nostrils, a nice brown trout on a Bloody Butcher. I held him a moment, admiring the size and shape of the body. His back was a rich green-brown colour, his belly yellow, flanks speckled with black and red spots. Such smooth scales. I let him go and watched him make a mad dash for freedom. Good luck to him. Also near Midleton, after a night of hard rain, an autumn brownie on a Black Pennell at the work station above Ballyedmond Bridge on the Owenacurra River.

A few choice specimens have surfaced on occasion from tributaries of the Lee. Worms did not work in the Glashaboy one rain-flecked day at a location near that deadly hairpin bend above Upper Glanmire Bridge. A kind man with local knowledge took time to put his rod down and saunter in my direction. "Try this instead," he advised, handing me a lump of Calvita cheese, which I ledgered in a small pool. Out jumped a rainbow, on the run from the nearby trout farm. From the Martin above Blarney Bridge, a small brownie on ledgered worm. As for the river that divides and haunts the city, the Lee, the waterworks weir out by the straight road is a productive spot. One hot summer's day, using an unknown fly, I landed a tiddler brownie, scales that sparkled in the sun, followed by a small fighting perch on a black and silver salmon fly.

We have travelled west out of the city, out of the county. As far west as we can go, to the Owenascaul River on the Dingle Peninsula where we caught seven wild Kerry brownies, including two for Barry, on Black Pennell and Blue Dun flies. That event occurred on the day before Pepé came into this world. We did not know about his imminent birth then. We were not to know about Pepé, and his subsequent love of fishing, until four and a half months later when he scampered into our lives.

So we are back where we started: fish are creatures hooked on memory. Fish are triggers to unleash the past. With their noses they eke out memories buried deep in silt. Unknown to us, they use their heads to nudge those distant, half-forgotten, half-submerged, parts of the human mind. We return, in our memories, to still waters. Waters that run deep, of course. And deeper still.

The still, deep waters above Inniscarra Dam. The day before we set out from Crosshaven on that boat trip with Denis to land all those mackerel, we cast maggots into the lake and returned over a dozen rudd. Claire landed one, her first fish. I can still see the brilliant red hue of its fins in her hands. Barry and I landed six apiece. The still waters of Curraheen Lake, a jewel of a reservoir near the city. Carp dive deep here, as do tench. The day was overcast, threatening rain. Wind ruffled the water as Barry and I fished quietly. We shared six rudd on floating sweetcorn. Next day we went to Turners Cross to see Cork City play FC Koln, Tony Polster and all, in the Intertoto Cup.

Still waters of the Lough. The stuff of memory: a ridiculous, circular fish-pond far too shallow; eight inches deep, standing *on* the earth not in it, constructed of household bricks slapped with cement, stocked by a nine-year-old boy with a net. A 1960s pond in a suburb of Cork. A 1960s schoolboy obsessed with fish.

We have a much better pond in Lusk these days. Bigger, deeper, made of moulded plastic, sheltered from the sun and overhung with plants. Over the years we have kept koi and all sorts of goldfish here. We once had a ghost koi called "Jaws". An oxygen-depletion incident robbed us of him. We purchase our stock now, but have experimented occasionally with minnow and stickleback, even flounder, netted from the Broad-meadows in Swords. A tench lives in our pond. He is rarely seen, burrowing deep in mud, his olive-green back impossible to detect from above. A "No Fishing" sign is strictly adhered to, under pain of enormous penalties. Another oxygen-depletion event occurred two years ago, much more catastrophic than the one that claimed "Jaws". It led to the loss of fifteen gold-fish. Three fish survived. The incident prompted the following story, "Dark Stripe".

After "Dark Stripe" comes "Undertow", another tale that owes its origins to the Lusk area or, more specifi-cally, to the beautiful horseshoe bay of Loughshinny, a carved jewel that sparkles on the coast of north county Dublin. Imagine what it would be like having never seen the sea before, and therefore rendered clueless as to the tide cycle, being trapped in a horseshoe bay with the water flooding in around your feet. What ter-ror would that strike in the heart? What religions and gods might spring from it? But before that last salute to the power of the sea, here is "Dark Stripe", a simple freshwater tale.

9

Dark Stripe

He scowled at me from his hospital-tank. The black stripe that ran the length of his tense gold body rippled with fury and despair. Pectoral and ventral fins thrashed water in a frenzy to declare how could I, or any pond-keeper worth the name, allow this happen to a world of my creation?

I stood with hands on hips and glared at corpses stretched on green grass. My eyes swooped over shades of red, orange, yellow, amber – creatures bred so carefully over many years. Adult and fry stared up. Anger mounted in dead-eyed glares. No prize fish, these; no Celestials, Redcaps, Pompoms, Orandas, Veiltails or Lionheads – lucky ones in safe indoor tanks. These were Comets and Common Goldfish; hardy varieties, aquarists say. Not hardy enough to withstand a near extinction-level event. I checked the torpid water with a net to see if anything else had lived. Dark Stripe was the only survivor.

I carried him indoors in his emergency tank. He seemed to turn for one last look at the polluted pond as I closed the shed door. There was no doubt in my mind as to what had caused the environmental disaster. If I hadn't been so caught up in the cares of the air-breathing world I might have acted responsibly and protected the pond from a build-up of toxic sludge caused by too much leaf-fall.

I switched on the shed light and positioned the hospital-tank above an aquarium full of Celestial Goldfish. Dark Stripe continued to stare accusingly through the glass: *how could you do this to my parents, my offspring, my lovers, my cousins?* I stared back, knowing that neighbouring pond-keepers would refuse refuge to my survivor, citing fungus and flukes and fear of outside influence. Dark Stripe was now a migrant seeking asylum in a foreign country where he would not be welcomed. I turned from the array of tanks and chided myself for such a thought. Stop being so sentimental. Go out and check the pond again.

I stood in the garden and stared at a pool of dead water. More swoops of the net yielded no survivors. Best course of action would be to leave the pond for now, empty it in late spring, clean it, start all over with fresh plants and new stock. I dropped the dead victims into the garden recycler – flashes of gorgeous colour in a dull brown bin. A memory came from decades past, from a pond much smaller than the one from which I rescued Dark Stripe.

"Don't smash the ice with your hurley!" My father had warned. "It'll send shock-waves through the water, startling the fish."

My childish mind was full of things aquatic, as well as stories of the *Tuatha Dé Danann* and *piseogs* to beat the band; a traditional upbringing steeped in the lore of history and countryside and the art of fish-keeping. Several days later, a small boy – I must have been nine years old – used boiling water from a kettle to make a safe and silent hole in a distress-free pond on a cold and frosty morning. Innocent days in a distress-free world.

Dark Stripe's fins, his magnificent pectorals and ventrals, began to calm down. His eyes grew accustomed to the light of the shed. His temporary tank contained no floor covering. Between the slats of the shelf he could see Celestials down below. They were stupid-looking; upward-facing eyes bred to gaze in homage to whoever might hand-feed them. Designer fish to please a Chinese Emperor by staring up in adoration. What really annoyed Dark Stripe was the way they looked up at him now and yet were pompous and pretentious, clearly wanting nothing to do with the newcomer in the shed.

There was no obstacle to seeing what swam in the overhead tank. Dark Stripe believed these fish to be Black Moors. He knew from his schooling that they were too delicate to survive in a pond. They have to be kept indoors because they don't like cool temperatures – mollycoddled weaklings. He also knew that if a Goldfish is all black, it cannot have normal eyes. It cheered him that the telescopic eyes of the Moors were on the sides of their heads and not staring down. Combined with the gaze of Celestials, that would have been a right old eye-sandwich. Some of the Moors had turned bronze, which reminded him again of his younger days as a fry in the nursery weeds where another thing they had taught him was that old Moors turn bronze with age. Dark Stripe felt sad then. Pond days flashed before him, especially memories of Red Tail: the pearl-like sheen of her scales; her deeply concave, pointed tail-fin longer even than her slender body. How shrivelled that tail looked as she lay dead on the grass where God-creature had placed her. Most of all he missed Red Tail's gentle, trusting nature. He felt agitated again. The water around him grew turbulent. He tried to concentrate on his surroundings to take his mind off bereavement.

Across from him stood tanks of ugly Toad Heads, Bubble-Eyes and various hooded varieties designed for fish shows. Dark Stripe felt sorry for these delicate species with their exotic bodies and bizarre finnage, and wondered if it was true that many of them were culled to produce specimens acceptable to the air-breathers. He shivered then, before settling down near the bottom of the tank. He wanted to dive deep out of sight of the airy world. He wished he could expel the poison of the pond from his mouth, gills and nostrils, just as he longed to keep sorrowful memories and loneliness from overpowering his head. Evening light faded. Darkness shielded him from the upward glares of Celestials, not from the fear and dread of what might befall him in days to come. He huddled in a corner and wished the night away.

I am glad my favourite lived. Why am I so fond of Dark Stripe? I don't know; he's just a fish. Appearances matter in the aquatic world and above it. Dark Stripe is a stunning fish even if of a common variety. I like him all the more because he had the strength to survive a cataclysm. Not only has he survived well in the month since the toxic event, he has thrived in his tank which I recently planted with *Vallisneria* and *Elodea*. I had hoped he might make his home in the shed but now realise it is cruel to confine him. You can put an aquarium fish in a pond and he'll feel liberated. Put a pond fish in a tank? It's like caging a wild bird.

It is late spring and the time is right for cleansing and re-stocking. I have come to a decision. I am abandoning the garden pond project. My decision is not taken lightly. I have always divided my time in favour of exotic indoor varieties and will concentrate on them in future. I can do without the carnage of another eco-disaster. I do not have time to maintain the delicate balance a pond requires. So what to do with my survivor? I could slip him discreetly into a friend's pond but that would be unfair on my friend and his pond – Dark Stripe may harbour some toxic residue which could harm a delicate ornamental environment.

Dark Stripe reminds me of my childhood, the folk-lore and fairy stories of the south. Perhaps it's because I had a striped fish like him in boyhood days when I smashed ice with a hurley. A common motif ran through the old folk tales I devoured back then. The motif of transportation – not in the physical sense – transportation of the self, the being, into an Other-world, the realm of the *Sídhe*, call it what you will. I still read a lot of the *seanchas*, the old myths, folklore and mythologies – reading and fish-keeping my bachelor passions.

Maybe I was trying to re-live childhood days when, unknown to my father, I once released a half dozen Goldfish fry into a nearby lake. I was trying to make up in some crazy way to Dark Stripe for the loss of his world, so I did the same for him by releasing him one foggy May morning into that same lake where I knew there lurked no nasty predators – just friendly Rudd, his cousins Carp and Tench – and maybe, just maybe, the descendants of small fry of forty years ago. If truth be told I knew my childhood fry could not have survived – they were too young and fragile – but I was a child then and a wise old adult now and Dark Stripe is a mature fish, and strong. Releasing him constituted an illegal act but I had to do it.

Fins quivered, not in anger, but anticipation. Tremors of excitement ran through him. God-creature had placed him in a new pond, but what a pond, a whole other world! Such weeds, whole brocades of them. None of that frilly *Vallisneria* stuff. Proper plants, and what depth! So many places to hide and spawn and ... hunt. Dark Stripe glanced around. He hid behind a forest of weed but soon emerged again, curiosity his new master. He felt himself transported and spellbound by his new surroundings.

Over coming days he explored every crevice and recess, each slope and shelf. He saw many creatures he knew already from pond-bound days: water fleas and bloodworms, caddis fly and mosquito larvae; parasites and scavengers. Frogs were familiar to him but the fish! He recognised Minnow and got a fright at first sight of Gudgeon. Soon he realised the Gud was just a harmless bottom feeder. Burnished bronze scales of Rudd appealed to him. He felt himself attracted to Carp, especially females. They looked at him in a funny way and snubbed him. He did not care. He was free and the world was new – he even leaped out of the water to catch insects.

He swam and he swam and he swam. After many darkenings of the water he found himself back where he had started. Shortly after one very bright sunrise he discovered an exit from the lake. Flowing water, the stuff of pond-nursery legend. He realised he was in what they call a stream. The stream broadened and joined a river. The current grew so strong he felt tingly all over. He let himself go with the flow and loved the sensation of running water, such an unstoppable rush.

He relished the slalom over riffles and glides but grew nervous when riffles turned to full-scale rapids. Then the river slowed and meandered in a series of large pools. He saw a juicy earthworm hang in the water and was tempted. The shadow of a God-creature on the surface sent him scurrying into the shade of the riverbank.

Soon the river broadened and became shallower, lacking in weeds. Dark Stripe was not used to gravel beds and felt a foreboding at being exposed in the open like this. The green-yellow livery of a snake-like creature snapped at him. He had never seen such rows of jagged teeth. He ducked and dived and just avoided the snapping jaws of what could only be a monstrous Pike. Dark Stripe scuttled behind some rocks, fearful for his tail and what might snap it off. He swam like the rapids for ages until the water became tangy and not to his liking. He had heard about this different type of water in among the nursery weeds one day, and knew it was bad for Goldfish. He also saw – growing *under* the water – the same plant, grass, that God-creature had laid Red Tail and the others on the day of the disaster. He knew then he was in a tidal flow and would have to turn back.

Thoughts of Pike did him no good at all. He swam stealthily in by the riverbank, aware that gold scales stood out like sparkling sunlight, eyes on the alert for telltale flashes of green-yellow leviathans that might lunge at him from anywhere. He found another opening, an exit in the riverbank, the outflow of a tributary different to the stream he had used to journey from lake to river. He followed this water for several dark-enings and brightenings, fighting the flow, keeping always on the look-out for predators. Eventually, the stream opened into another lake bigger than the one God-creature had released him in. It was also more inviting in that it had more crevices, shelves and slopes to explore, was deeper, richer in weed; the water was oh-so-fresh and the fish were friendly. Minnow, Gudgeon, Roach, Bream and Carp abounded.

One lazy going-down of the light when water was still warm with the heat-haze of sun and Dark Stripe had got to know the lake well, he saw a small fish, a female, in among clumps of sheltering plants. She was bronze-scaled with fins that burned a deep red colour. Dark Stripe gulped in a mouthful of water. She was beautiful and plump with eggs. She saw him and let herself sink to the sandy bottom as if inviting him to nudge her upward with his snout.

The rockery I planted last summer looks well. You'd never believe that a garden pond once lay beneath. On occasion these past twelve months I have wondered what befell Dark Stripe. I got my answer the other day when an angler told me he had caught a tiny Rudd, so he had thought. "Had the most peculiar lateral line ..."

"Rudd don't have lateral lines."

"I know." He scratched his head. "Must have been a hybrid. Looked for all the world like a lateral line, that tiny black stripe."

I nearly fell off my barstool. I asked him what size this fish was. He indicated two inches between forefinger and thumb.

I smiled. Dark Stripe was a solid four-inch torpedo when I released him. The angler told me where he had made his catch. It was my turn to scratch my head.

Back home I checked watershed maps and charts. The journey from lake to lake, as the crow flies, is five miles. For a fish, I ran my map-reader over the Ordnance Survey chart, it's nineteen long miles by the shortest route that I know of.

I folded my maps and charts and gazed out the window. A full moon hung like a Japanese lantern.

Somewhere out beyond the mountain, that same moonlight casts a sheen over the waters of a faraway lake. Perhaps, in the deeps, a fish is staring up wondering what lies above silvery ripples.

Swim well in your lake of new hope, Dark Stripe. You have been transported in the oldest and best sense. Float away from enemies. Find more females to chase; nudge their undersides with your nose to make them spawn. Make milt in evening shadows. If, like your offspring, an angler someday catches you, he also will scratch his head and wonder where you came from, and how you came to swim in waters free and clean and wild.

10

Undertow

Enormous eyebrows arched across a forehead that sloped up and back at an alarming angle. Not that Unga's eyebrows were a pair – they were so overgrown they met in the middle and hung like sparrows' nests over sockets so deep they resembled caves. A jutting jaw completed the profile of what looked like an ape.

As his eyebrows arched, Unga's mind overflowed with fear, bewilderment, joy and curiosity. For the first time he saw something he and his people had never seen before. In seeing it, everything became insignificant: three days pursuing elk; three days wandering farther from the settlement than the tribe had gone before; these things did not matter now. The excitement of the hunt paled compared to the thrill of seeing for the first time that tremulous, shimmering thing that lay before them, as awesomely impressive as the sky above: the sea.

Unga stared, mesmerised, deep blue eyes reflecting the greater blue before him. His gaze flitted from one end of the ocean to the other, from the nearest visible wave to the far horizon. He watched the sea glisten and heave, like a huge, breathing animal. It reminded him of meadow grass on a windy day. Instinct told him its movement did not signal malign intent. He stared for minutes before curiosity overwhelmed him. He began to clamber down the hill, conscious of his companions urging him to stand still. In a fleeting moment of near-panic, he realised he had advanced in front of Bronga.

Unga fell to his knees.

Bronga glared like a rogue elephant. He sprang forward and kicked Unga hard in the groin. Unga slumped to the ground. Pain shafted him like a spear. Doubling up on the grass, he clutched his burning testicles, fearful of what might happen next. Bronga towered over him as he lay face down, nose buried in mud, eyes screwed shut, expecting at any moment a second vicious kick.

None arrived. Satisfied that submission was complete, Bronga turned and walked away, urging the others to follow.

Unga remained prostrate until the last of his tribesmen shuffled past. Then it dawned on him like a sabre-tooth to the heart: because he had submitted, Bronga would have his woman when they made their way back to the caves. Simmering with anger and shame, Unga picked himself up and limped slowly after the others.

They came to the side of a stream. In the distance a horseshoe bay beckoned. At first their eyes were hooked on the expanse of water on the far horizon. At some distant point, shrouded in heat-haze, edge of sea and sky shimmered as one.

Bronga's attention was drawn to the nearer waters of the bay. The open ocean was boring; the immediate coastline more alluring. Down on the shore marching lines of white waves broke on golden sands. All around were high, rusty cliffs. To one side of the horseshoe, where cliffs were lower, a stream ran out to sea, reflecting the glare like a sun-bleached bone.

Whooping with joy, Bronga urged the others to follow him. He romped across the stream, splashing wildly. He ran to the edge of the cliff. Eleven primitives, including Unga, imitated his every move. They climbed down the rocks to where the stream cascaded into the bay. To their dismay the stream fed into an underground river flowing from a crevasse at the base of the cliff. River and stream combined to cut a channel deep and wide along one arm of the horseshoe, making access to the beach impossible and forcing them to keep in by the cliff.

Twelve heads flitted and bobbed. A dozen pairs of eyes darted and danced in all directions. Up at the lofty cliff, down in search of uncertain footholds, out at the wayward sea. Unga stayed well behind Bronga. When their eyes accidentally met, Bronga glared menacingly.

Unga averted his gaze, fearful of another attack. His leader growled and continued to lead the tribe slowly to where cliff surrendered to ocean.

The rock-face yielded abruptly to the sea. It did not slope gently; its jagged edge fell sheer into sand less than a man's length from breaking waves. Bronga came warily to within arm's reach of the lapping surf. To his left the river had swollen, disgorging into the ocean. In front of him, finger-lengths away, fading coronas of foam receded across the shingle. To his back, the towering cliff. To his right ...

The right-hand side of the horseshoe morphed into a motherly arm that cradled a little cove in the cliffs to the north of the bay. The cove nursed an almost perfect crescent of sand, long as a tree's shadow at evening time, surrounded on all sides by steep granite. Its only access was via the small strip of shingle separating the cove from the giant horseshoe to the south.

The primitives stood on this small strip of shingle, restless eyes flitting from the vast sweep of the bay to the restrained sands of the cove. Unga also stared. He saw again his shame at the hands and feet of Bronga. He knew there would be further humiliation when they returned to the caves. What Bronga would do to his woman didn't bear thinking about. Unga clenched his fists, angry at Bronga, angry at the tribe, angry at the ocean, angry at himself.

The tail-end of a vagrant wave stretched across the shingle and kissed the base of the wedge-shaped headland. It wet the tribe's feet before diffusing into sand. Afraid, they looked to Bronga for leadership. Seeing that the bay was cut off by the river, his decision was never in doubt.

They followed Bronga like a clutch of chicks to the centre of the cove. They cavorted in the sand like children let loose in snow. Unga forced himself to join in, his anger and shame eased by this new environment which drew him like a magnet to the strange world – half land, half sea – at the foot of the cliffs.

He saw warty rocks covered in crustaceans browsing on kelp and oar-weed, bladder and bootlace. In mottled pools of languid water barnacles opened their caps and waved their arms to catch food. Among nets and funnels of filter feeders he saw forests of sea-kale where predators preyed on mermaid's eggs; where hollows and whorls and gulleys were full of sea-squirts and slugs and cucumbers and sponges; where colonies of lampreys, polyps and molluscs were crawling and gliding and gorging and, betrayed by bubbles, foraging and fornicating. In salt-laden worlds he saw angels and monsters, squid's ink and crab's blood. In recesses in the cliff he saw polished stones, mammoth's bones, shark's tusks. When he looked again at the sea ...

He saw footprints swallowed by advancing waves. Alarmed, he signalled to his tribesmen. Where there was sand there was water, where there was shingle breakers pounded into the rocky promontory around which they had walked. One look at waves banking along the face of the headland and the primitives knew there was no going back. They looked to Bronga, fear in their eyes, grunting for guidance.

Bronga went to look for footholds in the high granite wall behind them. He found none. The twelve made their way along the base of the cliff in search of safety. Down one arm of the cove they hurried until fear of waves forced them back. Down the other side they scurried, quicker this time. Again they drew a blank. No craggy path to freedom, no escape from their diminishing cove.

Slowly, inexorably, the sea consumed the sand where they stood. Fearfully, they watched surging swells accelerate onto the ever-shrinking beach.

No longer a cohesive group, they resembled a ragbag running to and fro seeking pathways of escape. Some were brave and tried to keep the sea at bay with rocks. They stopped throwing when their arms grew tired or when they realised how futile their action was. Others cowered at the foot of the cliff, wailing at impending doom.

Unga stared at onrushing waves. He stood motionless, seething at this latest indignation. Bad enough the hurt and humiliation of the morning, death now faced him in the shape of a great, heaving, land-eating monster. Spurred by rage and fear, he looked around.

All that remained from base of cliff to breaking rollers was a sandy crescent narrower than a man's shadow.

Of the twelve, only Bronga and Unga remained clear-headed. They searched for a route up the overhanging precipice. Bronga tried to climb a vertical rock-face. He hauled himself above Unga's head but groping fingers lost their grip. He fell to the ground, his ankle giving way under his collapsing body.

The honeyed taste of revenge surfaced in Unga's consciousness. He towered over Bronga, feeling the urge to kick and crush. In the end he didn't even gloat, merely glowered at his fallen leader. Bronga looked up, body and pride torn, the failure of the climb and the pain of a broken ankle frustrating him until he was reduced to the level of a hunted animal whimpering in the face of death. Resigned to their fate, the others watched timorously as Unga stepped to where there was an imperfect line of seaweed and fragmented shells. The sea lapped his feet. He wanted to be taken first. He had suffered enough already. He saw his past; he saw his future – no woman, no pride, only anger and fear. A deep-seated rage uprooted the fear in his mind. Roaring demonically, he stood like a scarecrow, arms outstretched, bellowing at the waves, exhorting them to let the tribe survive.

Time stood still.

Wavy lines of froth undulated against the row of weeds and shells. Then the sea itself stood still until, incredibly, it began to recede. In half an hour the water had retreated the length of two men. Only then did Unga's arms fall from their messianic pose. Hours passed.

The strip of shingle around the headland lay exposed again.

Hooting with delight, the others followed Unga out of the cove along the river up to where the stream cascaded into the bay. Only then did Bronga, hobbling painfully on broken ankle, surrender leadership. He fell to his knees and licked Unga's feet. As the others rushed to follow his example, Unga looked at the sky and smiled. On his face the searing heat of the sun; on his feet hot, clammy tongues of adulation; in his mind the power of the retreating sea – a raw, shimmering power he could harness and use to his advantage. He looked down. Eleven tribesmen lay prostrate before him.

Several generations later, when the tribe became dominant in their region, they had one golden rule: whoever came within sight of the sea was to turn back immediately under pain of death. They had one god. In his honour they erected a stone statue in the centre of their main settlement. That statue stood for many generations, arms outstretched.

11

Legends of the Lough

I find myself back at the Lough. I am lured to this place the way a salmon is drawn by the pull of the natal river. Mine is an inexorable pull, preordained and not without purpose.

That church on the hill up around the corner no longer leans overhead, threatening small boys and small girls with authority and oppression the way all Cork churches used to do. The city spires have shrunk, small steeples on my seldom visits to these streets and roads. We have liberated ourselves from that binding and blinding carapace of claustrophobic collar bones. Eyes of passersby no longer shine with piercing whine of holy pictures. Ghosts of old wives do not bother me now. I let ghosts of the past to their devices, and me to mine. For years I wore this city like shoes a size too small; hobbling, crouched in doorways, my young untainted back against the wall of walls. Looking over my shoulders at who might see and talk about me: wives of merchant princes in ermine coats in Thompson's for morning tea; craw-thumpers, gossipmongers, guardians of the faith. The old Thompson's is gone now. So are the craw-thumpers and guardians of the faith – most of them, anyway. We have matured. A lot has changed.

The Lough remains the same.

I sit on a bench on one of those irregular Friday afternoons when I drive over early from Waterford to angle a few hours before heading to Turners Cross football ground to see Cork City play. The inscription on the waterside bench reads: "Dedicated to the memory of Nellie O'Donovan (1927-2008) for whom the Lough was a special place." I don't know who Nellie was but I thank her for the generosity of her seat, and she was right – the Lough is a special place. I sit here now contemplating a lifetime's worth of fish. Almost a quarter of a century has passed since that summer's day on Mountcharles Pier re-ignited my passion for angling, which in turn lay another quarter century on from netting thorneen, redbreast, pinkeen and roach in this sacred water. A half century, give or take a year or two, when I have never felt the need to land a 20 pound salmon or a 250 pound shark. I feel no desire to start trophy hunting or scalp hunting now. Fishing has never been a numbers game to me. It's about much more than that. The only number that counts is one. Please God, give me just one.

This part of the Lough is open water, far away from the island. Perhaps not the best fishing spot. Closer to the southern end is more productive. I prefer it here. Wildfowl tends to stay away. Birds and ducks congregate in flocks in the narrows up around the slipway. Nellie's bench is close by a tree; handy for shelter from the rain. Not many visitors to the Lough make it over this far. They stay at the southern end, feeding birds and ducks.

Barry and Claire no longer fish with me. They have grown up and have other things to do. Barry admits to six huge halibut in Alaska one recent summer, so all is not lost. Perhaps we'll fish again before our spools run out. I sit alone now, stretching my arms along the backrest of Nellie's bench. A sudden chill comes from somewhere, perhaps from overhead, making me conscious of how much of my own line is spun, how little is left.

A pole-fisher, buzzers and rod-rests and shiny equipment coming out his ears, sits a couple of pitches away to my right. Eyes hidden behind silvery shades, a tent erected on the grass behind him – an overnighter, probably an Englishman in search of monster carp. His pole stretches telescopically over the water. He stares intently at his float, turning his nose up at the ill-equipped fisher to his left. I have two rods out; net unfolded on the kerb three yards away, ready for action.

Old ladies, dog walkers, mothers with young children, pass me by, as do old men. Some men are solitary. Others congregate in small shoals beneath trees like fry sheltering under weeds, waiting. They sit on benches longing for the sun to cross the yard-arm before they walk through the doors of the Hawthorn Bar. Some cannot wait that long. Joggers run the oval path that surrounds the ten acres of the Lough; each circuit a mile, so they say. Healthy runners bounce smoothly as they move, others lope along. Sweat-soaked skin glistens in sun that breaks through a sky filled with high and mid-level cloud. Cirrus and altocumulus, hints of a herring-bone day – not bad for late April, though the smell of heavy showers hangs in the shape of darker clouds coming down on cool northerlies.

Observation mode has me in its grasp. I put on my pair of shades, all the better to see with. A pair of stride walkers pass by, jerking elbows and hips. They wear chains of digital trance, earbuds that link head to pocket devices so smart they hold playlists of thousands, yet no outer sound penetrates. Not the hurly-burly of kids in the playground nearby, not the sound of birds that sing and dance in branches overhead, not even the great *comhluadar* of city sounds – airbrakes squealing on the number 14 bus as it stops over on the far side, a motorbike revving past, rising hubbub of traffic on the Lough Road, chatter of passersby – all speak in magical whispers to a wind that stops and listens to the sound of leaves falling in autumn, the beat of swans' wings in summer, shrieks of schoolgirls in spring. Even winter has its quiet sounds when all of nature appears to sleep.

Nowadays so many people choose to ignore natural and environmental sounds by wearing links to smartphones, tablets, pads and pods – these invisible helmets are a modern sorrow, a virtual affliction that drops outer sounds like tears shed on the inside, falling in silence, evaporating. It's the same on public transport these days. Sit anywhere on a bus and watch a girl fingering her screen for miles; virtual friends, likes. Student two seats ahead; white wires, song after song. Across the aisle incessant chatter of unlimited calls and free wifi. Young men watch movie downloads or game with one-touch fingers. Tablets and pads scrolling, scrolling, scrolling. The windows of modern buses are fogged with fug of access. No apps for the passing world; these buses never stop for apps or for anyone. Terminus approaching.

Model boat races took place on the waters of the Lough back in the sixties. Grown men used to sail pond yachts from the approximate location of Nellie's bench all the way over to the far side, where the Lough puffs out at its widest. The little yachts sailed gracefully like swans with wings erect and open to the wind. I wonder do the races still exist? Speaking of swans, here comes one now – a Mute, a fine specimen. He regards my floats with suspicion, then ignores them by giving both a wide berth.

The swan's invisible paddling creates a moving script, a capital V traced in inky green water, reminding me of the V my floats will trace when I pull them in, hopefully with a heavy load at the end of the line. I think of our two Vs, mine and the swan's, twin hieroglyphs of man and beast – fisher and wildfowl. We stare ahead, eyes and hearts full of shared impulses – instinctive, primal – intent on the same pursuit, one unified goal: what the Lough holds beneath the surface this calm spring day. I am no longer watching people. I am in consort with nature, with the birds and the fish. The swan glides on. I form my lips into a puckered circle and exhale, making a sound that back-answers a cooing pigeon invisible in the trees, and consider that if reincarnation does exist, if it is more than mere question mark, we could do worse than, when the soul is unfleshed, return in the form of the majestic swan now gliding by.

I lean forward on the bench, eyeing my twin floats. The orange stick dangles a sweetcorn bait, the red bubbler supports a ball of bread. The floats barely undulate on mirror-like water. Hunger rumbles in my stomach. Two hours until I get to Lennox's on the Bandon Road for chips – and fish, naturally. A pint in the Horseshoe or the Beer Garden before the game. Tonight's match crosses my mind. A home win is vital because ...

Green water stirs in the peripheral vision of my right eye. I sense this shift in the cosmos before seeing it. Another letter V, horizontal to the shore, is being written in the aqua-sphere. A bandy-legged V, subtle, more like a small bow wave. Not a bird. Not wildfowl. Not a toy yacht. Something glistens. A momentary glimpse of gossamer-like latticework a good fifteen inches behind the apex of the V – a dorsal fin breaks the surface. I notice the shadow in the water around the bow wave. The breath stops in my throat. An enormous carp is cruising, out for an afternoon's surface swim, gliding casually parallel to shore – and coming within casting range. I glance to my right. The pole-fisher has, unbelievably, failed to spot this colossal quarry floating by.

I am off the bench like a predator striding quickly, purposefully, to the water's edge, eyes tunnel-visioned now; grassy green shores of the Lough cease to exist. Joggers, dog walkers, mothers with strollers, hurlers on the green, children in the playground to my right, old ladies feeding birds from bags of bread up at the slip, pensioners colluding for a drink, visiting pole-fishers with upturned noses – they all disappear. The island of the Lough falls off the edge of the world, as do the swans, ducks and birds. The sky no longer looms blue and white overhead. I only have eyes for what is heading my way. Sound also vanishes, as though traffic on the Lough Road and Hartland's Avenue ceases to move. I can no longer feel the warmth of the sun on my face. All my senses have gone to my hands, to the rod I now hold.

The float on my lightweight lies too close to shore. The carp rod's payload of three sweetcorn kernels on a size 6 hook is too far out. I reel in the line hastily until the kernels lie along the glidepath of the gigantic carp, but am concerned because they hang low – eighteen inches deep, maybe twenty – and he might swim over them. I spool in the lightweight five-footer and quickly examine the ball of bread to make sure it has not disintegrated and fallen off the size 8 hook into the mud below. The bait looks secure, so does the shot to keep it down a mere four inches, which should match this client's snout-depth. A glance to my right confirms that the fish is holding course, heading by in a matter of seconds. I cast out, praying my nerve will hold and that I get the distance right. Concentration works: the bread plops where I want it, off to the left. I reel in close to where sweetcorn dangles. Peripheral vision is no longer required; the target fills my eyeline now, coasting gently, dorsal again breaking water. I glimpse the broad expanse of his back. My God, he is huge. He glides over the sweetcorn as if it were not there, then slows.

Time elongates, elasticates, goes on forever. Fisherman freezes as fish slows. The red bubble-float wobbles, moves a fraction to the right, then a fraction to the left. The angler also wobbles, knowing the fish is examining his bait, nudging it with that great nose, whiskering the bait with his barbels, feeling the soft promise of fresh bread in his mouth. Go on! Take it, nibble, swallow the damn bread! A hint of dorsal fin breaks the surface, then vanishes. What if they're not feeding? My chest tightens at such a heretical thought. Oh Jesus, carp are mysterious beings with inner ignition that needs to be switched on before they eat. How to switch on that inner feeding engine? Nobody knows, especially the nervous angler standing on the shore. It seems to depend on a combination of season, water temperature, windspeed, and light – and who knows what else.

The float settles. The carp is no longer interested. My heart sinks along with the body of the fish I am losing. For a tense moment, which again goes on forever, nothing happens. My eyes are drawn left, expecting to see evidence of a bow wave head away from my baits. I see nothing, and nothing happens endlessly, so it seems, until the surface around the floats rises as though a massive disturbance, a seismic aquatic event, is taking place in the water beneath the bubbler. I hope he's turning, I pray he's turning. I *know* he's turning, but is he sounding for those deep kernels, those glossy, yellow, low-hanging fruits of sweetcorn? The tip of the orange stick shortens as it dips ever so briefly, then shoots up again. He had them in his mouth but spat them out. My nerves are starting to fray at this stage. A giant carp playing around like this is too much to bear. The skin on my face starts to crawl with aching tension.

Again, nothing happens. The Lough stands still as though time itself has frozen solid – as rigidly and icily compacted as the winter of '63, the winter of 10/11. Both winters combined could not have solidified this world more severely. For seconds, nothing stirred. Nothing at all. No fish swam, no birds flew, no joggers ran, no dogs walked, no children played. A plane flying in to Cork Airport hung suspended in the air, motionless above the Lough. Time stood still for so long there was a silence between the tick of hope and tock of expectation, a silence long and neverending where it seemed all hope and all expectation had faded to nothingness. The fish had gone. Then the orange stick-float vanished. It did not sink from view. It simply winked out of existence as though it had been whipped down out of sight. For a moment I stood, an imbecile on the shore, not crediting the evidence of my eyes. Then I heard and felt the run-off of line from the spool, tingle of an electric take in my hands.

How to tell that my fishy friend knew he had a hook in the sweetcorn sitting behind his fleshy lips? Only one way to find out – but when to apply pressure? Strike too soon and the line may snap, or the hook might pop out. Fail to strike and he will be so far away the line will tighten and snag around a submerged obstacle, perhaps a hidden underwater branch, of which there are many in the Lough. All the textbook information on what to do in a situation like this lay stored in the back of my head, and there it remained. What little I could recall in the pre-battle heat of this encounter, and battle there would surely be, was that, yes, it's good to give line. Let him have his head, but not too much. There was only one thing for it. I closed the reel-gate and jerked the rod. It was as if the line had attached itself to an immovable locomotive engine that had fallen off the rails. Dead weight. I knew I had to open the gate again in case the line broke.

What had been a gentle run-off turned into a literally screaming reel. The line disappeared so fast and hard I swear I saw steam rise off the spool. Then I saw the carp's bow wave, a tsunami tearing out into the middle of the Lough. His huge purple back surfaced briefly, size and colour of a tree trunk. Then he sounded. What to do? What to do? Feed him more line? He'd get a hundred yards away! Close the gate again and try to halt him? The gut had a breaking strain of twenty pounds and I already knew, from the evidence of my eyes and the strain in my hands, that he far outweighed that. One glance at the spool confirmed what I was already too aware of – line was running out.

I closed the gate and prayed. The rod jerked forward. I held on to the butt-end the way a cowboy hangs on to the horns of a runaway bronco, nearly tripping headlong over the kerb stone at the edge of the path and falling into the water. Somehow the line held firm and so did I. Silence and stillness descended. I balanced on the kerb. I could feel the weight of him out there, lying low. This could be a long waiting game. Give a little line when necessary, reel in every now and then, but always spin in more than given out, and drag him that little bit closer. So the textbooks say. I began to remember expert advice now. Off he went on another run away to the left, no bow wave this time, then a watery surge fifty yards away. He had turned sharply to his right.

The line fell slack. My jaw dropped. Either the gut had snapped or he was coming back towards me. I reeled in, a belly-churning slow reel, breath coming hard and fast. I did not want to tug too hard in case he was still on – a sudden jerk might break the line or unhook him. I found from somewhere in the deepest pit of my lungs the air to make a forlorn sigh. He was gone, I was sure of it. Then the line straightened and cut through the water creating its own miniature bow wave, the little V-wave of every fisher's dream. The Lough exploded twenty yards out. A giant carp rolled on top. What a specimen! I knew a former Irish record carp, a mere three ounces short of thirty pounds, had been taken here in this very water. Legends of the Lough attest that there are thirty-pounders here, maybe even a forty-pounder. If that was the case, I had him on the line, right in front of my eyes, rolling and roiling and why wouldn't he? Dammit, he was away again, a runaway number 3 bus headed towards Ballyphehane Church and taking my precious line with him.

By some miracle the line held. I coaxed him shoreward once more. Give a few yards here, take more there, certain the line would snag or snap or get tangled in the five-foot rod's line which lay foolishly beneath the surface ready to spoil the retrieve. Pulling him in was such hard work. Finally, I had him ten yards out, glanced at my net and realised it was much too small to bag him, then watched him splash again – what a tail – and make another run, shorter this time, not as fast.

Maybe he was tiring, but it still felt like I had at the end of the line a giant Mahseer fish from India, or a Great White from Australia, or a dolphin from the Caribbean. Whatever this behemoth was, it was not for giving in easily. Another huge splash, another run. Then I reeled in slowly, evenly, weight of expectation heavy on heart, head, wrist and arm.

How would I land this huge fish with my inadequate net – a *trout* net, for God's sake? I glanced around. There was no one left at the Lough. Dog walkers, mothers with strollers, old men, joggers; all had gone – even the swans had disappeared and the playground lay empty. An upward glance revealed a huge thundercloud dark and brooding, spilling its load. Where had that come from? I hadn't even noticed the rain. The pole-fisher was nowhere to be seen – perhaps he'd gone to the Hawthorn? I saw his net then; a proper, elephantine carp net fit for the biggest carp ever caught in Ireland. The net lay on the grass near his tent. I shuffled slowly sideways towards his fishing perch, the bend in my rod straining under the weight of what I hoped to catch. More in hope than expectation I called out, "Help, I need a hand."

A baldy head emerged from the green canvas tent. The pole-fisher that had been sheltering from the rain read the situation straight away and understood his fellow-angler's predicament. "Must be a biggie!" he smiled as he grabbed his gargantuan net.

I couldn't believe my luck – a helping hand when most needed. The carp was close now, my rod an archer's bow drawn to an impossible angle. I braced, expecting the line to break at any moment, or the rod to split. I had the carp within five yards. The urge to step in and wade out proved almost irresistible. I had never seen an angler do that at the Lough. Wading in was normal practice at other lakes, I knew, but my thoughts were interrupted by one last mad bid for freedom. "No, not now, please don't slip off the hook now," I pleaded to some unknown entity.

This immense lump of fish rolled one last time and pulled away, but the struggle was getting to him, too. He only made a few yards before the pull of my arms dragged him back slowly to within five yards again. And closer still, the pole-fisher bending forward, arms outstretched. He swooped the manta wings of his huge net through the water under the great belly of the fish, then lifted it up, up. Water swirled from great swishes of the carp's tail. Brush-strokes of his body broke the surface. Then the net surfaced also, surrounding him.

His vast, fully scaled body glistened golden in the sun, or would have, but that dark cloud still spilled rain. I was soaked, but did not care, and was exhausted, though I felt no tiredness. There was nobody around to witness this stupendous catch except a pole-fisher and a rod-merchant. I struggled to hold the fish in my arms as Bill took photos with my mobile phone. My tiny spring-weight only goes to twelve pounds. No worries:

Bill had the latest digital weighing gauge, of course, to go with his buzzers and all the other razzmatazz gear he had. We placed the fish carefully in the weigh-bag, making sure we knew the weight of it first. When we had done our subtraction we shook our heads in amazement and disbelief. The fish's weight was forty-four pounds, six ounces. We weighed him again to be sure. Same result. I held the fish one last time and reckoned he could have been almost fifty years old. I kissed his big, broad head. His large, dark eyes stared at me, disbelievingly. The last thing I wanted to do was drop him, such was his regal weight, on to the concrete path that surrounds the water. Four hands were needed. Bill helped me release him back into his home. We watched the fish lay still a moment. Then, with a great swish of that fan-like tail, he swam out into the Lough, where he still lives and reigns, I hope, the King of all the Carp.

I thanked Bill profusely. I would have never caught that fish without his skilled netting. I promised to pay for a creamy pint to be perched for him that night on the counter of the Hawthorn. I left the Lough then, drove for my fish and chips at Lennox's before parking the car at the usual spot near the football ground in Turners Cross. The City team were in predatory form that night. As lean and hungry as any fish that ever swam in the cool waters of the Lough, they tore a weak opposition to shreds in a mighty thrashing. I missed some of the goals though they all took place in front of my eyes. My concentration lay on earlier events this star-studded day. I drove carefully to Tramore afterwards, arriving around the usual time of 11.00 p.m.

Though I still have the phone photos as proof, and Bill's address in Bristol to back up my claim, I have resolved not to submit for a new Irish record. I want to be consistent. Fishing is not about numbers.

I slept well that night and dreamed I had waded in after the gigantic carp. An ill-advised move, but only on the surface. The fish had regained all its strength and stubborn sense of purpose. It dragged me head-first towards the island in the middle of the Lough. In my dream I would not let go of the rod's butt-end. Pulled along, I skipped over the surface like a flipping mad stone or a water-skier gone over, flaying the surface with helpless limbs and hanging on, hanging on. The fish was so strong! My face skimmed the waves. Water cascaded around my head and into my nostrils, a horrible gurgling feeling up my nose. I felt sure I might drown yet, strangely, no panic set in. On and on the carp pulled as though reeling me in, diving so hard and deep that soon I was under water.

I saw gnarled clumps of bog-oak rooted to the muddy bottom of the Lough in stumpy imitation of elephant's feet cut off in their prime. Between these dark stubs, tree trunks lay in heaps. Branches snapped and twisted in serpentine lengths. Broken ends of rotting trunks displayed rings so numerous the great age of the trees was obvious even to my incredulous glance. It was dark down there – I don't know how I could see the rings, never mind count them. My eyes had become magical, and then looked inward: I realised that the rings of my own life had also multiplied – I was being dragged hard through water and through time. The great spool was reeling in. My line was running out. Pulled along on this grand tour of an exotic world, I found I had developed gills and web-like folds of flesh between my fingers.

The submerged trees were the petrified remains of long dead forests. Between these ancient remains, skid-marks lay etched in mud. I wondered what could have caused these lines in the sedimentary levels but the King of the Carp pulled ever harder, ever quicker. He gave so little time to think yet I felt no fear and saw that the legends of the Lough are true: under the island are spires and steeples, domed roofs and scalloped balconies peopled by strange, fish-shaped creatures with human faces, though the heads are more aquatic-looking than ours. These exotic creatures waved to me with fin-like arms.

Beneath the city, a small dungeon lay buried in the mud. The bars of a window protruded from the silt revealing the prisoners within. I knew instantly that this was a jail only for fraudsters and exploiters, and therefore knew what had caused skid-marks in the silt. These were the trails left by the tails of slippery eels and pin-striped sharks as they were hauled off to jail. Most of the sucker fish, bottom feeders and other parasites in suits had been put behind bars, too. The denizens of the Lough had got it right: they lived in a city without ostentation, ownership or exploitation. I could tell from the smiling faces of the creatures on the balconies that these were citizens of a realm that was content and just, a society without greed and corruption. What a fair and equitable world this underwater Lough was. For a moment I wished things were the same in the airy world above but deep down knew that could never be.

Next thing I knew I was wading in the mud and sediment of shallower waters. I perched my backside on the kerbstone that surrounds the Lough and hauled myself out by pressing down on my hands and heaving my legs up and over onto the path. I stepped ashore in front of Nellie's bench, sopping wet like a landed fish. There was no sign of my rod. It lay beneath the waves now, a gift to the underwater world and those who dwell therein. I breathed in the sweet air of the Lough through mouth and nose. I checked my cheeks. All traces of gills had vanished, as had the folds between my fingers. I squeezed those fingers together to make sure I was awake and was tempted to really pinch myself. The dream was over and I knew the day had come to draw a line. Time goes and finality beckons. A mallard that stood under the tree beside the bench gave me a most peculiar look with a sideways cast of steely eyes. He was a wise old fowl – he knew where I had been, what I had seen beneath the surface, and what I must do now.

I bit my lip and took a size 2 hook, my biggest and sharpest, from out of my tackle bag. Its barbs split my fingers as I set to work. With the business end of the hook soaked in water from the Lough and blood from my bleeding fingers, working feverishly I inscribed the following words in the soft wood of Nellie O'Donovan's bench. The words are still there, carved in small, neat, life-soaked letters, the calligraphy of the Lough itself. The message is simple. It reads:

I will never return. D.M.